Each month Harlequin publishes 12 new novels: six in the "Harlequin Romance" series and six in the "Harlequin Presents..." series.

 Each Harlequin novel is a beautiful love story — inordinately interesting, intriguingly informative, excitingly entertaining — without the overtness or violence so common in many forms of entertainment today. Harlequin Books take you to exciting, faraway places — places where engrossing, believable characters face real love situations.

 You will find yourself quickly drawn into the story and will be reluctant to put it down until the fascinating, romantic plot is finally resolved.

 You will enjoy Harlequin Books, just as millions of other women like you have for years.

Other titles by

SARA SEALE
IN HARLEQUIN PRESENTS

Other titles by

SARA SEALE
IN HARLEQUIN ROMANCES

Many of these titles, and other titles in the Harlequin
Romance series, are available at your local
bookseller. For a free catalogue listing all available
Harlequin Presents and Harlequin Romances, send
your name and address to:

HARLEQUIN READER SERVICE,
M.P.O. Box 707,
Niagara Falls, N.Y. 14302

Canadian address:
Stratford, Ontario N5A 6W2

SARA SEALE

to catch a unicorn

Harlequin Books

TORONTO • LONDON • LOS ANGELES • AMSTERDAM
SYDNEY • HAMBURG • PARIS • STOCKHOLM • ATHENS • TOKYO

Harlequin Presents edition published June 1975
ISBN 0-373-10097-3

Second printing June 1975
Third printing December 1976
Fourth printing March 1977
Fifth printing November 1977
Sixth printing January 1978
Seventh printing January 1979
Eighth printing September 1979
Ninth printing June 1980

Original hardcover edition published in 1964
by Mills & Boon Limited

CHAPTER ONE

SHE nearly missed the train owing to misjudgment of the time it would take a taxi to get from Earl's Court to Paddington, and pushing through the ticket barrier in mounting panic, and with only minutes to spare she found difficulty in getting a seat at all in the crowded compartment. She left her luggage in the corridor where it had been dumped by a surly porter who showed no inclination to be more helpful, and began a dispiriting expedition through coach after coach, stumbling over suitcases, bumping into passengers bent on the same search, enquiring angrily of herself why such simple matters as catching trains, dealing efficiently with taxis and porters should invariably elude her otherwise normal capabilities.

Cleo would have said: "Because you daydream, silly Laura, and don't have enough spunk to assert yourself when it comes to a pinch."

Cleo, of course, would have been right. Laura did not consider in all fairness to herself that she altogether lacked spunk, but her cousin did not understand where the difference between them lay. Cleo, with her sloe-eyes, vivid looks and inborn reliance on the good will of others, had no need to assert herself, neither was she given to the sort of daydreaming that would interfere with her immediate comforts.

"So sorry . . . excuse me . . . so sorry . . ." Laura murmured as she stepped on people's toes or squeezed past bodies reluctant to move for her, and finally tripped over an unobserved suitcase and fell sprawling in the corridor at the feet of a young man propped indolently against the door of a nearly empty carriage.

"Oh, buckets of *blood*!" she exclaimed, reverting to an oath of her schooldays, and staring up at the man who was already stooping to help her to her feet, thought that the absurd expletive was not inappropriate. He had the swarthy look of a pirate, his black hair curled with an exuberance which drastic barbering could not altogether control and his dark eyes were bold and adventurous and, at the moment, bright with amusement.

"I do apologise," he said. "I shouldn't have left my belongings strewn about in the corridor. I hope you're not hurt."

"I could," she retorted with a spurt of defiance to cloak her disadvantage, "have broken my leg! I'm not sure I haven't!"

He was kneeling beside her now, and his hands went, uninvited, to the knee she was gingerly feeling.

"I don't think so," he said with a grin as she hurriedly withdrew the leg from his exploring fingers, and he helped her up and started brushing her down, the amusement growing in his eyes.

"You have three freckles on the bridge of your charming nose—did you know?" he observed.

"Yes, I knew," she answered shortly, "and I expect there's a smut on my face, and my hair's a mess and I can't—*can't* fight my way back again down all those frightful corridors."

"Why try? If you can't find a seat, come in here," he said, nodding towards his own compartment.

"It's first class," she objected, and felt gauche when he laughed and opened the door with a flourish.

"Who cares?" he retorted. "I'll soon sort the ticket-collector if he makes trouble. I rather enjoy scenes when it's a question of one's rights."

Laura thought this was probably true, judging by his buccaneering looks, but she was exhausted by her fruitless battle down the length of the train coupled with a recent bout of 'flu, and the thought of having to stand in the corridor for the next five hours of that interminable journey to Cornwall weakened her resistance.

"All right," she said, and sank thankfully into the unfamiliar comfort of a corner seat, reflecting that this was the first and probably the last occasion she was to experience the cushioned well-being of first-class travel.

"Well," her new-found acquaintance observed, settling himself opposite her, "your misfortune is my gain. I was resigned to hours of boredom. How far are you going?"

"To Merrynporth, a little place in Cornwall. I have to change, I think."

"Merrynporth? Yes, you change at Truro. Do you know the West Country?"

She shook her head, aware of a fresh alertness in his frank appraisal of her, and moved a little uneasily. That bold scrutiny, which she was beginning to think held a shade of mockery, could become embarrassing and she glanced with relief at the other two occupants of the carriage who, apart from a brief disinterested glance upon her arrival among them, had retired behind their newspapers with the polite dissociation from their fellows common to British travellers.

The stranger saw her covert look and grinned wickedly.

"What unladylike thoughts you have," he said, and the grin grew wider as he saw her blush.

"That," he observed with interest, "is almost a lost art."

"What is?" she asked, unguardedly.

"Blushing. You must be very young."

She was in fact still young enough to resent that embarrassing betrayal of colour, and she replied defensively:

"I'm twenty, a—a responsible age, and I earn my own living."

"Do you indeed? What doing?"

"Selling flowers in one of those expensive little shops where nothing is ever fresh. At least, I was till they went broke. I mostly packed the orders, though, and filled the vases. Window arrangements were the skilled jobs."

"Of course! I can see you among your flowers, rather like a slender stem yourself, and that serious, pale little face a muted echo of the—er—creamier variety of blossoms, if I knew what they were."

Now she knew he was laughing at her and she blushed again, this time with indignation.

"You clearly have no conception of work in a flower shop with your hands in and out of icy water and your complexion more blue with cold than a muted echo of

7

anything," she said tartly. "Do you always make such extravagant remarks on first acquaintance?"

"Always. It usually pays off," he replied with outrageous impudence. "You have a smut on your face and your hair's distinctly windswept."

He grinned unkindly as she rummaged in her handbag for lipstick and compact as he knew she would, and idly assessed her possibilities as he watched her making repairs. She was not his type with that pale, wedge-shaped little face which seemed swamped by eyes that were too big and too lacking in guile for comfort. Her hair was mousy and probably afforded her dissatisfaction in its refusal to obey the more sophisticated rules of current fashion, but there was, all the same, something rather beguiling in the way it fell in innocent casualness about her rounded forehead and slender neck.

"Have you quite finished?" she asked suddenly, bundling her belongings back into her bulging handbag.

"Finished?" He was unused to being caught out in a deliberate inventory with such a lack of coquetry.

"Weighing me up—my looks, I mean. Cleo says I have no vanity, and it's probably true, but you're stuck with the face you're born with, so why worry?" she said with calm detachment, and he laughed.

"Well, you're a refreshing change, if nothing else, Miss—?" he paused suggestively, and because Auntie Flo, even though she disapproved of chance acquaintances, had brought her up to answer questions politely, she replied obligingly: "Laura Smith—and it really *is* Smith."

"Is it, indeed? And who is Cleo?"

"She's my cousin, and that's where I'm going—to help out with her little boy while she's staying with her new-found in-laws."

"Really? In Merrynporth?"

"Well, no, I don't think so. Merrynporth is the nearest station, but they live in a house called Penzion out in the blue somewhere."

"Really?" he said again, and she became aware that his interest seemed to have quickened, resulting in a

8

rather puzzling gleam of devilment in his alert black eyes.

She was about to ask him his own name when the ticket collector made a sudden appearance, and in the scene that followed she either forgot or decided belatedly it was best to remain in ignorance, for the young man's behaviour certainly lived up to his buccaneering appearance. He was arrogant and impudent by turn, uttered outrageous opinions of British Rail and its public servants alike, and Laura, blushing furiously again, hastily found the excess fare to end embarrassment, indignantly refusing the brash stranger's offer to foot the bill.

"You enjoyed that," she accused him when the man had slammed the doors on them and gone on his way. "You were just putting on an act to make everyone uncomfortable."

"Why not?" he replied, unabashed. "Come and have lunch," he said. "I'll treat you."

"Oh, no, I couldn't possibly," she protested, remembering belatedly her Auntie Flo's strictures on scraped-up acquaintances, but he shook his head at her.

"Too late for proper pride and decorum—we're practically old friends by now," he said. "Besides, you wouldn't allow me to pay your fare, although I insisted you stayed in this compartment, so the least I can do is buy you a lunch. Come on."

It would, she thought, salving her conscience as she took her seat opposite him in the restaurant car, have been churlish to refuse, besides which she was hungry.

She wholeheartedly enjoyed her lunch and the wine he insisted on ordering; the warmth and chatter and hurrying waiters made her feel rich and cherished, and the strange towns and fields and little homesteads flashing by the windows revived a pleasurable anticipation of this unexpected holiday among strangers.

Her companion seemed unusually interested in her destination and was attentive in topping up her glass as the level of the wine sank.

"I'm curious to know what's bringing you to Merryn-porth," he prompted. "To look after a child, you said?"

9

"Penzion. Merrynporth's the station," she replied meticulously. "My cousin's nanny walked out at the last minute, you see, not liking the idea of being buried alive with no telly or cinemas and things—*you* know! So Cleo asked me to help out as my flower shop has gone bust and I was between jobs, and it was an excuse for a holiday."

"A holiday doing nursemaid?" he interrupted sceptically, and she frowned. How explain to someone who did not know her that when Cleo asked a favour it was difficult to refuse, that acting as temporary nursemaid to Nicky was a pleasure rather than a chore, that a break from the dull routine of earning a living was indeed a holiday, especially in such unusual circumstances?

"You don't understand," she said, and one black eyebrow shot up in expectant enquiry.

"Then why not elucidate? I scent some sinister motive behind all this. Are you sure you haven't got involved with white slavers or the drug traffic or something?" he said with mock seriousness, and she laughed.

"Nothing more sinister than a dead family feud—at least, I hope it's dead," she said. "You see, my cousin Cleo and I grew up together—at least, we didn't exactly do that because there's nearly six years' difference between us, so she was grown-up and with strings of young men when I was still a schoolgirl . . . I was brought up by a maiden aunt after my parents died and Cleo's parents were in India, so when she was at school in England she used to come to us for holidays . . . Cleo and Auntie Flo never got on very well, but the money for her board helped a lot because Auntie Flo wasn't well off. Cleo, of course, was very bored with our quiet provincial life, but to me the holidays were exciting when she came to stay, and I suppose I must have had some sort of a schoolgirl crush in those days . . . Cleo, you see, was everything that I wasn't; glamorous, assured and, to me, fabulously sophisticated, which, when you're still in your early teens, seems the ultimate of ambition. And then she got married, and that's really the start of the story. She made a runaway match when she was only nineteen with

10

a dashing young man called Troilus Trevayne—isn't that a wonderful name? I never met him because they lived abroad and Auntie Flo and I lost touch . . ."

"Trevayne?" he interrupted again. "The Trevaynes of Penzion?"

"Yes, do you know them?"

"I know *of* them."

Laura beamed on him happily, feeling that this might almost constitute an introduction.

"Oh, then you can tell me about them—prepare me for what to expect. Have you got pirate ancestors?" she asked him perfectly seriously, and he laughed and topped up her glass again with wine.

"You were telling me, if you remember," he retorted, and now his bold eyes were bright with mockery.

"I don't know much, really, except that there were three sons and their detestable old father living in this house, Penzion. There's a family business which has been handed down from father to eldest son — a mine or a quarry or something — and the second son, Troilus, was engaged to some dreary girl the old father picked out for family reasons. This was all nearly seven years ago, of course, so I'm never really very clear about the details — anyway Troilus cocked snooks at his papa and ran away with Cleo to Australia, and that started the family feud."

She paused a little breathlessly to concentrate on her food which was growing cold, and her companion replenished his own glass and said:

"The prodigal son was cut off with the proverbial shilling and traditionally emigrated to the colonies, and till the day he died the bitter old man had no idea he had become a grandfather. The eldest son inherited as was to be expected, the black sheep, Troilus, was killed in a motor-racing smash, and though he had obviously left a widow, it must have come as a surprise that he had also left a son."

She looked across at him with widening eyes.

"You seem to know the story already," she said, sounding disappointed, and he grinned.

"I come from the same parts. Penzion affairs are pretty widely known and old Zachary—*de mortuis*—

was a by-word with his fanatical obsessions and family feuds," he said, and her enthusiasm in relating a past history which was no more to her than something read in a book of adventure seemed diminished.

"I suppose so," she said, and had a fleeting impression that this dark stranger was better acquainted with the Trevaynes than he implied. "They sound a rather spiteful family."

"Oh, yes, spite runs in the blood, so the gossips say —spite and a goddam pride."

"Not exactly cosy"

"Cosy! Is that what you expect from pirate ancestors?"

"Well, I expect I made that bit up," she said, a little sheepishly. "I used to enjoy tales about buried treasure and pieces of eight, and bottles of rum and things, when I was small, and these Trevaynes sounded larger than life with their brawls and their grudges and their story-book names . . ." She broke off as the train dashed into a tunnel, remembering how long ago those three picturesque names had caught her fancy; Dominic, Troilus and Peregrine . . . names, she had thought in her schooldays, that belonged to high adventure, the names of crusaders or swashbuckling sea-rovers.

"This Dominic—is he fair-minded?" she asked, and he cocked an eyebrow at her.

"The predatory overlord? Well, that you'll have to find out for yourself, won't you, Miss Laura Smith?"

"Why do you call him that?"

He shrugged, and his mouth twisted in a wry, half-bitter grimace of amusement.

"Perhaps, like you with your preconceived notions, I think it fits," he said, and grinned afresh when she replied rather primly:

"I don't think you should try to put me off with local gossip when I'm going there as a guest. Dominic Trevayne answered Cleo's letter very civilly when she wrote to tell him he had been an uncle for five years, which might, you must admit, have put anyone off, taken on the hop, so to speak. He invited them to stay in order to get acquainted, which doesn't look, does it, as if he intends keeping up this silly old feud?"

"Feuds can provide meat to get your teeth into when the fires begin to burn low, and the flames need fanning to keep one alive," he said, and though she knew he was laughing at her again, there was something in his voice and eye which caused her a twinge of foreboding.

"That's nonsense. If you need a grudge to give you an interest in life then you're better off dead," she said in such governess-like tones of reproof that he flung back his head and laughed.

"What a literal mind, Miss Smith Have some more wine," he teased, but she placed a hand firmly over her glass.

"It's made me talk too much as it is," she said. "My Auntie Flo would be scandalised."

"Then don't tell her."

"I can't very well, she's been dead two years," said Laura with such polite apology that he laughed again.

"You're either a very naïve young woman or a bit of a minx," he said, and Laura, who would have liked to be taken for a minx but knew very well she was, upon occasion, distressingly naïve, coloured again.

"Not a minx, evidently, how disappointing. Do you live alone now Auntie's passed on, or does the fascinating widow provide a home?"

"Cleo? Oh no—we tried sharing a flat for a bit when she first came home, but it didn't work, and I went back to my hostel. It suited Cleo better to have me on tap to baby-sit for odd evenings."

"I don't doubt it did. Are you a doormat, Miss Smith?"

"Certainly not! I'm very fond of Nicky and it's never a chore to do things for him — he's left too much to nannies. Whatever Cleo's new in-laws turn out to be it will be good for the little boy to lead a normal family life for a bit, and if his uncle only takes a fancy to him—"

She broke off, and the spark of devilment was back in his eyes.

"Don't bank too much on a sentimental streak in the head of the house of Penzion," he said with a dash of impatience. "From all I hear, the gentleman's pretty much on the beam if he suspects any funny business. I hope your cousin's equal to him."

"Cleo's equal to anything, and what do you mean by funny business?" she said, rather regretting the freedom with which she had discussed her cousin's affairs with a stranger, and he gave her a placating smile.

"Nothing, probably. There's funny business *and* funny business, isn't there? How come you're not travelling together?"

"Oh, Cleo and the boy are already there. I got 'flu at the last minute, so they had to go without me," Laura said, and stared out of the carriage window, remembering how annoyed Cleo had been at the unfortunate hitch to her plans.

"Well, I'll have to cope myself for a few days, I suppose," her cousin had said crossly. "I daren't put my newly discovered in-laws off in case they change their mind, but I'll be a wreck by the time you come—Nicky wears me to shreds."

Laura smiled to herself remembering how unfitted the lazy, delectable Cleo was to contend with the responsibilities of motherhood. Nicky had been born too soon to afford his irresponsible young parents anything other than a liability and a hindrance neither had wanted so early in marriage. Nicky was, thought Laura, her smile changing to a sigh as she dwelt for a moment on the waste of an unwanted child, a very manageable small boy considering all things.

"Having second thoughts?" her companion asked, hearing her sigh, and wondering what outlandish bees were chasing round in her bonnet now, but although she shook her head, she was not sure. She felt dispirited, and unsure of what welcome awaited her the other end, and curiosity had changed to irrational foreboding.

"It hardly matters what I think, does it?" she said. "Cleo's the only one they're interested in, and Cleo can cope with most situations."

"She sounds a formidable young woman."

"Not formidable—just born under a lucky star and knows most of the answers."

"And you, of course, don't. Hero-worship's a mug's

game once you've outgrown your teens, my dear Miss Smith. See you don't get trampled on."

"I've no intention of being trampled on," Laura retorted coldly, resenting his personalities a little too late. "And since you've never met my cousin, your advice is rather impertinent."

"How prim you suddenly sound," he mocked, and she giggled, dismissing her tardy dignity, but aware all the same that she had been behaving with a rather lamentable lack of discretion.

"I think," she said, trying to sound as if chance encounters were quite usual in her experience, "I would like to go back to the carriage. Thank you for entertaining me, Mr.—?"

He did not, however, oblige by furnishing her with a name, but gave her a considering look and called for his bill.

The daylight was already going when they regained their compartment and there would soon be nothing to see from the windows but scattered lights twinkling from the darkness and the passing glimpses of nameless stations. Presently the dark stranger left the carriage and disappeared down the corridor, and did not reappear until the train was pulling into Truro and she, half asleep herself, began collecting her belongings with the slight feeling of panic which beset her when having to change trains at a strange junction. It was a relief when the dark young man took charge of the luggage, remarking that they would still be travelling together, and if he smelt rather unmistakably of whisky, Laura was thankful for the obvious familiarity he had in regard to the correct platform for the stopping train which would take her the rest of the way on a small branch line to the coast.

"Are you going to Merrynporth too?" Laura asked as the little train pulled jerkily out of the station.

"I'm getting out two stops before, so don't get carried on," he replied.

"Carried on?"

"To Land's End—or it might be Hades with the dark Pluto waiting for you at the other end."

"How absurd you are!"

"Am I? But you're in Cornwall now, Miss Laura Smith. Strange things can happen in these parts. Don't say I didn't warn you."

"Warn me of what?"

"Of the pitfalls, perhaps, which could await unsophisticated little girls who still believe in buried treasure."

"I'm not," she replied coldly, "as unsophisticated as that."

"No?"

"No."

She was beginning to fight a losing battle with sleep. The long journey following on too brief a convalescence had, she supposed, proved unduly tiring, and her fellow traveller's personality had ceased to charm. She closed her eyes and began to drift into oblivion.

She slept fitfully, jerked to consciousness each time the train stopped at a station with shuddering violence, until she began to wonder if she would reach the end of her journey in one piece. She was aware every so often that the dark stranger opposite watched her, and it must, she imagined uneasily, be the erratic lights, or perhaps it was the effect of the wine which lent his face a suggestion of malevolence and gave a horned twist to his eyebrows.

When the train stopped again, her companion jumped up suddenly and pulled down the small case which seemed to be his only luggage, at the same time giving Laura's heavier suitcase a shove to greater safety on the rack above her head.

"This is where I leave you, Miss Smith. Pleasant dreams, and don't get carried on to Hades. Yours is the next stop but one," he said, and favoured her with the now familiar derisive grin as he swung himself on to the platform.

"Goodbye—and thank you for my lunch," she called after him, remembering that after all he had never told her his name.

"Not goodbye, we shall meet again," he shouted back, and was gone, leaving behind him the strange impression of a buccaneer who could possibly claim other and more sinister connections.

"Absurd!" muttered Laura, and slipped back into sleep until the subsequent stop warned her that she should be getting her belongings together.

Someone opened the door for her and heaved out her suit case, and she stumbled on to a deserted, ill-lit platform. For no reason at all her legs gave way under her and she went down on the rough surface, hitting her head sharply on her suitcase as she fell.

The next thing she knew she was sitting on a station bench, dazed and not at all sure that this was not part of a dream and she had indeed arrived in Hades where, any minute, Pluto might materialise in a cloud of sulphur.

"You're quite likely delirious," she chided herself, speaking her thoughts aloud, a bad habit which had been much deplored by her Auntie Flo.

"Talking to yourself?" a voice beside her enquired politely, and as she jumped, then turned with her head spinning in protest, she thought for a wild moment she had raised the devil by her thoughts.

The dark stranger who confronted her was alarmingly familiar and, in her befuddled state of mind, seemed to be a combined manifestation of the traveller on the train and the more sinister counterpart of her dream.

"How can you appear like this?" she demanded indignantly. "How can you come out of nowhere?"

"What an odd reaction to a perfect stranger," he replied, shooting up a pair of black, horned eyebrows. "Who did you think I was?"

"The devil," she answered without any thought.

CHAPTER TWO

A GUST of wind blew between them, making her shiver, then he moved into the feeble light of one of the station lamps and she saw her first impression had been wrong. He was older, less attractive than that other stranger, although the same buccaneering illusion persisted, making the dark, dominant features familiar; then he turned to meet her full face and she saw with a small sense of shock that his left cheek was marred by a curiously shaped scar which drew one corner of his mouth into a very slight twist of permanent derision. The devil, indeed, she thought, still bemused by that crack on the head, and was unsurprised when he addressed her by name, for supernatural knowledge was only to be expected.

"Well now," he said with gentle irony, "no wonder you're looking at me with such wide-eyed apprehension. I haven't, I assure you, suddenly materialised to carry you off to the nether regions, but to take you home."

"Home?"

"To Penzion. Didn't you expect to be met?"

"Oh! Then—then you're a Trevayne?"

"Naturally, even though you seemed to expect a more satanic courier. I'm Dominic Trevayne."

"It's the same thing, really—at least, I mean my *original* idea, pirates and things—the devil came later —" Laura replied somewhat incoherently. "I was dreaming, you see, and the man on the train got mixed up in my dream and grew horns, so when you appeared, the likeness confused me—the man, not the devil, I mean." She thought his expression was somewhat sardonic as he replied:

"Very illuminating. I'm relieved the likeness turns out to be more mortal than infernal. It would seem you must have met my brother. He was expected by this train, too. but he doesn't appear to be around."

"He—your brother—got off two stops back," she said, aware now that her acquaintance on the train had been enjoying a private joke of his own at her expense.

"Oh, I see. His usual date at the Bunch of Grapes, one presumes. Peregrine was doing his stuff, I imagine —didn't he know who you were?"

Laura sighed.

"Oh yes, he knew. He picked me up in the corridor —literally, I mean—I fell over his suitcase. And then he insisted I travelled in his compartment because I couldn't find a seat and we got talking and it was a long journey, and I saw no harm in it—besides, he bought me lunch," she finished defiantly, and he cocked a quizzical eyebrow at her.

"It's scarcely my place to rebuke you, Miss Smith, even though I might share your aunt's misgivings," he said, and she recognised the familiar note of mockery that was an echo of the younger Trevayne. "Did you find him attractive? Most women do."

She was not prepared to identify herself with a nameless string of easy conquests for her host's amusement and merely observed a trifle coolly that the younger Mr. Trevayne might have seen fit to acquaint her with his identity since he already knew hers.

"Oh, that wouldn't be Perry's way. He likes to keep them guessing, and he doubtless found the journey dull," he replied carelessly.

She did not much care for the implication that her engaging fellow traveller had merely been relieving boredom, but her head was beginning to ache and she felt in no shape to argue. Dominic Trevayne stood looking down at her with absent attention for a moment, then asked if she felt sufficiently recovered to walk to the car. She got to her feet without replying and he picked up her suitcase and began striding along the platform.

"Sorry," he said, and paused as he heard her stumbling after him. "Am I going too fast for you?"

She was tired, the eventful journey ending as it had was hardly a restful follow-up of 'flu, and her head felt as if it must be swelling visibly.

"I'm beginning to think your brother was right," she snapped with irrational inconsistency. "He told me I wasn't at all fitted for a life among pirates and smugglers and predatory overlords."

That certainly stopped him in his tracks and he turned to look at her.

"Did he, indeed?" he observed mildly. "What a curious picture he must have presented of Penzion."

"The picture was mine, I suppose," she said a little crossly, aware of how childish she must have sounded, "I'd made my own imaginings, you see. The Trevaynes had always sounded as if they had pirate ancestors."

"And predatory overlords—where did they come in?"

"That was your brother's invention. I wouldn't know what he meant."

"He meant me, my dear Miss Smith, and was not, I think, indulging in adventure-book fantasy, like you. You might as well know now that the accident of becoming head of a family breeds resentment, for you'll find it out for yourself."

He had spoken with such unexpected bitterness that Laura drew back a step, thinking that her preconceived notions of the Trevaynes had not been so misplaced after all. They were all alike in one thing, these two brothers; they shared a streak of tough arrogance and possibly other traits besides.

"Don't look so alarmed, I was only warning you," he said on a gentler note, and she smiled a little uncertainly.

"Your brother warned me, too—of the pitfalls that might await unsophisticated little girls who still believed in adventure tales. You seem to be a very prophetic family," she said, and he laughed.

"On the contrary—you'll find us a hard-headed, down-to-earth lot, I'm afraid. We haven't much time for romantic fancies at Penzion. Here's the car. You'd better get in while I shove your luggage in the boot," he said, and she felt rebuked for foolishness like an importunate child.

"I realise, Mr. Trevayne," she said as he settled himself in the driver's seat, "that I must be making a — a rather idiotic impression. I'm neither a little girl, *nor* completely unsophisticated—so *I'm* warning you."

"Really? Well, that's fair enough; now we're both

warned," he said with the same amused indulgence his brother had shown, and she was dismayed to discover that she was experiencing an ignominious desire to weep. He was unbearable, she thought, in his assumption of adult superiority, and totally without his brother's charm to cloak a sting with humour. He turned suddenly, one hand already on the ignition key, and looked down at her with a new expression which might have been mistaken for tenderness.

"Head aching?" he asked, and the unexpected solicitude was her undoing. The tears escaped despite herself, and she turned her face into his shoulder because, what with the pain in her head and the absurd fancies which had led to her making a fool of herself, any shoulder was better than none.

"That," he observed with a comforting lack of embarrassment, "is a much more natural reaction. Cry away the ache and the tension, Miss Laura Smith. My shoulder is reassuringly human, even though you did mistake me for the devil."

"I didn't really," Laura gulped. "Perhaps I was concussed, or something."

"You're rather absurd and not at all my idea of a nanny," he told her, and watched her forehead wrinkle in perplexity.

"I'm not a nanny at all," she said, sounding surprised, "I'm only helping out with Nicky because I'm between jobs and Cleo thought a holiday would be good for me. Besides, she was rather stuck when the proper nanny walked out."

"Oh, I see. Then you've no experience of looking after children? I understood that the boy had been your charge for a little while."

"Only at odd times. I baby-sit for Cleo whenever possible, and Nicky took to me. He's a good little boy when he doesn't feel he's neglected.

"Neglected?"

"Not *neglected,* of course, but—Cleo can't always be with him; she likes to be gay."

"Gay?"

Laura glanced up at him, belatedly aware of the reserve in his two interpolations. She had forgotten for the moment that this was her cousin's brother-in-law, the man it was so important to impress with the just claims of his only nephew. Dominic Trevayne might well have that native chapel streak in him which Cleo had said was common to many Cornishmen, and take the view that a widow of only one year's standing should scarcely have thoughts bent on frivolity.

"You shouldn't blame Cleo for—for a natural inclination," she said gently. "She's very attractive, still young, and has a great zest for life. You wouldn't want her to mourn for a past that's over and done with, would you?"

"Is it done with?" he asked on a note of coldness. "I understand that my sister-in-law feels the past owes her something."

"Nicky, not Cleo. He's of your own blood, after all. Don't you feel he has some claim on your family?"

"Upon my soul!" he exclaimed. "You've been well primed, whatever your position in Cleo's ménage. Just arrived, a stranger in our midst, and already you take me to task on my family obligations."

"It's not my place to take any of you to task," she said, "but *you* brought the matter up."

"So I did," he replied, and the humour seemed restored to his voice. "I'm glad to hear you remember your place, Miss Smith, though I'm beginning to wonder what that is."

Observing the shifting play of light over that rather harsh profile as the car passed out of the station yard, Laura reflected that her charming cousin would be well advised to walk delicately with Dominic Trevayne, for she did not think he was a man to succumb easily to feminine wiles and evasions. A hard-headed, down-to-earth lot, he had warned her, just as his brother had warned her of pitfalls . . . Well, thought Laura, drifting into snatches of uneasy sleep as they seemed to speed endlessly through the darkness of narrow lanes and twisting moorland roads, the pitfalls, if any, would scarcely be lying in wait for her, a passing intruder in Trevayne affairs, and Cleo could well look after herself.

Her impressions of her arrival at Penzion were, afterwards, a little confused, though the vast hall she found herself standing in while Dominic Trevayne fetched her luggage from the car only served to heighten her first fancies. Firelight flickered on great presses and display cabinets and armour, and other dim shapes reflecting light from glass and metal and polished wood; shields and trophies of war and the chase hung on the walls, and a massive chandelier swung so high in the vaulted roof that it afforded little light. Barking dogs, shouting voices, merged with the banging of doors and a rhythmic dull booming which must, she supposed, be breakers beating against the rocks somewhere near, and gusts of wind blew in at the open front door with eerie sounds of wailing until her host came in and shut it behind him with a slam.

"Well," said Dominic with a tinge of mockery, observing her air of awed surprise, "is it the expected setting—devils, pirates, predatory overlords?"

"Yes," she said, unaware in the pleasing corroboration of her extravagant fancies that he was laughing at her.

He turned to one of the several doors which opened on to the hall, and Laura followed, thankful that Cleo would be waiting for her, impatient no doubt to hand over responsibility for Nicky without much thought for the personal reunion between them, but familiar and with both feet comfortably on the ground after rather a surfeit of improbability. At the same moment the sound of distant barking broke out again, and more voices shouting, and Dominic gave an impatient exclamation.

"Blasted dogs! Amos has let them out again, I suppose. Come in and get warm while I go and see about that tea," he said, and she went past him into a long, low room which, though without distinction and plainly furnished, had, after the museum-like grandeur of the hall, an air of comfort and homeliness. Cleo, Laura guessed, would sniff at the masculine clutter, the indifferent paintings and the roughly patched tears in rugs and upholstery, legacies, probably, of generations of undisciplined puppies, but lights blazed with cheerful if redundant extravagance from every available fixture, and great logs were piled high on the cavernous granite hearth.

"Hul-*lo* . . ." came Cleo's husky voice in lazy greeting, and Laura saw her cousin stretched out on a sofa by the fire, looking sleepy and thoroughly at home, a trolley laden with bottles and decanters and glasses of all shapes and sizes at her elbow, just as though she had lived here always instead of barely a week.

Laura ran across the room to kiss her, grateful for a return to normality, and even when Cleo drew back, warding off an embrace which might, she said, still be infectious, that, too, was encouragingly familiar.

"I don't mean to be off-putting, darling, but I can't afford to risk going down with something as unbecoming as 'flu at this juncture," she said with a conciliatory smile, and stretched out a hand for the half-empty glass beside her. "You *do* look washed out, poor sweet! I hope you're feeling strong enough to cope with Nicky — he's quite worn me out since we've been here, and if it hadn't been for Bella—"

"Who's she?"

"Bella Spain, housekeeper-cum-impoverished friend of the family—a very odd bod at times, my dear. It's said that she was one of old Zachary's mistresses in days gone by. She's been here ever since Mrs. Trevayne died when Peregrine was born and virtually brought the younger two up. She's not too sure about me yet, but she's sold on Nicky."

"Nicky—how is he?" Laura asked eagerly, and wished it had not been too late to go upstairs and tuck him up.

"Hasn't settled down too badly considering everyone's strange to him, and of course he dotes on the oddities of this preposterous house. Incidentally, that perishing brat of mine isn't being at all co-operative; he seems to have taken a scunner to the only uncle who's important to him. I hope you'll be able to wean him to a more tactful state of mind now you're here."

"Your brother-in-law might seem alarming to a child at first," Laura said slowly, remembering her own impressions as he had turned the scarred side of his face to her in the unkind glare of the station lamp.

"Yes, he hasn't Perry's charm, of course. What did you make of brother Dom?"

"I don't know yet. We didn't get off to a very good start. I mistook him for the devil." Laura had thought to amuse her cousin by recounting the vicissitudes of the journey, but Cleo frowned and poured herself another drink.

"You aren't, I hope, going to be tiresome while you're here," she said a little sharply. "My newly-discovered in-laws may look romantic like the old-fashioned he-men of fiction, but they're not at all given to whimsy."

"So I've been told already," Laura said, feeling snubbed, and was relieved when Dominic reappeared carrying a laden tray of tea and set it down beside her.

"Dom, I helped myself, I hope you don't mind?" Cleo said with a charming but not very serious suggestion of apology for having presumed on his hospitality. "You were so long fetching Laura that my tongue was hanging out — shall I mix you one?"

"Thanks, but I'll have a whisky and help myself," he replied, and she made a wry little face at him.

"Sorry—I should have waited to be asked," she said. "It's your fault, really, for making me feel I belong here. Penzion's the first settled home I've had for years —even if it is only temporary."

"Well, you're entitled to think so if you can stomach our slapdash ways," he replied pleasantly, unstopping a decanter and pouring himself a moderate measure of whisky. "As for waiting to be asked, you ought to know by now none of us stand on ceremony here."

"Oh, that's nice. Now I shall know we're not treading on any corns if Nicky and I think of this as home," she said cosily, and moved her very decorative legs to make room for him on the sofa with a small silent gesture of invitation.

Laura poured and drank her tea, aware without rancour that they had forgotten her. She was so used to her cousin's unfailing gift for monopolising male attention that she would have been surprised had she been noticed. Cleo's husky overtones were warm and familiar, but what she said passed unremembered as did

25

Dominic's replies. His was a dark voice, matching the dark Trevayne looks, where his brother's had been light brown with shallow depths, Laura thought fancifully, and jumped when Dominic suddenly asked Cleo a question.

"By the way, why didn't you tell me you were cousins?"

Cleo's mischievous, sloe eyes opened wide.

"*Didn't* I, Dom? Well, I suppose I thought you knew. But of course you couldn't be expected to know anything about either of us since we've never met or corresponded until now, could you?"

"It was Troy who cut himself off in the end," he reminded her. "I wrote more than once after the old man died."

"Did you? Troy never said, or perhaps he never got your letters — we were always moving on and you know what hotels are about forwarding. To be honest with you we often didn't leave addresses — importunate creditors and other embarrassing encumbrances — Troy's, of course," Cleo said lazily, and gave him a look which plainly intimated they shared the same knowledge of the dead Troy's failing, and that she for one took a worldly and tolerant view.

"Where's Perry?" Cleo added, tactfully trailing a less controversial red herring. "I thought he was due in on Laura's train. If they'd known in time they could have travelled down together."

"They did," he replied with a certain dryness. "Perry, needless to say, got off at St. Mewan, presumably for a date with the latest floosie. He'd made good use of his time with your cousin, I gathered, but didn't see fit to disclose his identity."

"And Laura, of course, gave hers away in the first five minutes and probably talked a lot of indiscreet nonsense. I suppose, knowing Perry's line with susceptible females, he filled you up with blarney to pass the time and you fell for it."

"He filled me up with more wine than I'm used to, which undoubtedly loosened my tongue," Laura answered coolly enough, and caught Dominic's quick little glance of amusement.

26

"I don't doubt, since your cousin is capable of standing up to the devil and demanding his business, she's equal to dealing with less alarming situations," he said to Cleo. "Now, as Miss Smith has finished her tea, perhaps you would like to take her upstairs and show her where she's to sleep and the general layout."

"Oh, for heaven's sake call her Laura! In a madly indirect fashion you could claim her as cousin, I suppose," Cleo said, and sounded really cross, but she got to her feet, if not very graciously, at least with a belated sense of satisfaction that she was being tacitly assigned the rôle of hostess.

Before they could get out of the room, however, the door burst open and a pack of yelping dogs bounded into the room, followed by a very large, angry woman brandishing a saucepan.

"Devils! Ingrates! Thieves and scullions!" she boomed in a voice like a cracked bell. "Where is Amos, Dominic? Why can't he learn to keep the brutes shut up in the kennels? They've stolen the joint I'd prepared for supper and there's not enough left even to make into a stew. It's too much . . . too much!"

Cleo looked unperturbed, if a shade disgusted, but Dominic simply stood and laughed and encouraged the dogs with cries of "Worry-worry-worry!"

"Really, Dom, you can be as bad as Perry at times! Poor Laura is looking as dazed as if she had walked into a madhouse, as well she might," Cleo said with a touch of sharpness, and his laughter died.

"Your cousin will have to get used to our ways if she's to settle among us for a time," he said, and the old touch of hauteur was back in his voice. A reminder, Laura thought, that however boyishly he might choose to behave at times, it should not be forgotten that he was head of the house and unaccustomed to censure.

The angry woman scooped up what was left of the joint with the utmost *sangfroid*, deposited it in the saucepan and advanced upon Laura.

"How do you do, dear child? You don't look at all suitable for a nanny, too thin, and too young—oh, *much* too young," she said as though nothing had happened.

"We were," observed Dominic still with that air of

27

stiffness, "misled about Miss Smith's position here. She is Cleo's cousin and very kindly just helping out in a domestic emergency. Laura, this is Miss Bella Spain, our trusted friend and very respected housekeeper."

"Oh, in that case—" Miss Bella Spain said, and left it at that with what Laura was to find was a familiar trick of inconclusiveness.

She was, thought Laura, finding her hand taken in a warm but—after dealing with the joint—greasy clasp, a woman of indeterminate age, rather overpowering on first impression. Her hair, piled up in complicated and untidy swathes, was a most unlikely and violent shade of red, her proportions, once Junoesque and splendid, had now tended to sag, and her old-fashioned dress, inadequately protected by a tiny and frivolous apron, was spattered with ancient stains of grease and gravy. There was, nonetheless, something gracious and reassuring about Miss Bella Spain, and Laura said shyly:

"How do you do, Miss Spain? Nicky knows me very well, so you needn't have fears on account of my thinness or my youth. Do you think I could see my room?"

"Of course. Cleo, take your cousin up while I get these shockers back to their proper quarters. Is the head giving trouble, Laura?" said Dominic.

"It aches a bit," she said, grateful that he had remembered, and he told her firmly that she was to go early to bed and he would send up something to help her sleep.

"You'd better have something upstairs on a tray, and if you're not better in the morning I'll get the doctor. We don't want to find we've ignored something serious, do we?" he said, beginning to chivvy the dogs out of the room.

Laura was asleep long before her host's promised sedative was sent up, and morning found her quite refreshed. She sat up in bed to take curious stock of her new quarters which last night had made only a dim impression. The room was reminiscent of the old-fashioned bedrooms of country hotels, only very much larger; the bedstead high with a profusion of brass knobs and scrollwork, the massive furniture ill-matched but adequate for most needs, the marble-topped wash-stand and the faded sprigged paper on the walls reminders of a much earlier decade. Auntie Flo would have been quite at home here, thought Laura, and felt a little embarrassed by the advent of Miss Bella Spain bearing a laden breakfast tray.

"How are you?" she enquired in her booming voice, depositing the tray with scant attention to comfort or security on Laura's knees.

"Quite recovered, thank you," Laura replied. "You shouldn't be waiting on me, Miss Spain."

"Just this first morning. Your cousin," she went on, drawing back the curtains with a violence that provoked a shower of dust from the pelmet, "was remiss in not explaining who you were. We thought you were the little boy's nanny, or I would have seen you had a better room—not that this one was ever assigned to servants, you understand; they have their quarters in the other wing—not of course that we have any servants, but you follow, I trust. Eat your breakfast, dear, before it gets cold.

Laura, who did not follow at all, obediently began on the breakfast which, doubtless owing to a prolonged journey from the kitchen without the protection afforded by covers and tea-cosy, was already cold.

"How is Nicky?" she asked, since Bella showed no signs of going. "I really should have been up earlier to take him off my cousin's hands."

"No need as it's Sunday—no need at all," Bella said, adding as if that explained it, "The boys won't be at the works, you see."

It seemed odd to hear the two very adult Trevaynes referred to as the boys and did not throw light on Nicky's apparent lack of requirements, but Laura was eager for information about the family's business.

"What does the quarry produce?" she asked, but Bella looked vague.

"Granite and stone for building — sometimes the most beautiful quartz, only of course that hasn't much value — china clay, naturally," she replied. "I'm really not at all clear about it, dear child — Dominic will explain it to you. Now, you were asking about the little boy. We are strange to him still and he keeps asking for Moo-moo — a pet, no doubt, or even a toy?"

"Oh, that's me," said Laura, with a surge of warmth that she had been missed by someone. "It's Nicky's own invention — I don't remember why. Hasn't he — hasn't he made friends with his uncles?"

"Peregrine, yes, but not Dominic. The scar, perhaps, frightens him."

"How did he get it—the scar, I mean?" Laura asked without thinking, and felt reproved for curiosity when Bella looked vague and replied as if she had not heard.

"Peregrine, of course, has a way with children and women alike. It comes of not caring sufficiently to make himself unpleasant, you see. Troilus was the same. You are not like your cousin at all, are you, dear child? Dominic fears you may have a weak chest, but he's accustomed, of course, to a more robust type. Your cousin, now, could well be Cornish. She has great attraction, has she not — what used to be called in my day *beauté du diable* — so much more descriptive than glamour-puss, or a dish, I always think."

At the same moment Cleo herself popped her head round the door to enquire for Laura's well-being and Bella smiled upon her with absent appraisal.

"Are you going out with the boys, dear child?" Bella asked. "Sunday's the day they like a good tramp with the dogs."

"Perry's not up yet—he didn't get back till all hours from his junketings last night," Cleo replied. "Dom said he'd drive me up to the village for cigarettes when the pubs open. I'm not madly enamoured with good tramps myself. Will you be able to take Nicky over, Laura?"

Bella, beaming vaguely upon them both, observed that in Zachary's days Sunday mornings were spent in more profitable occupations than walking or driving, and their women knew just what to expect, and then sailed out of the room, the uneven hem of her outdated skirt trailing after her like a train.

"What an extraordinary person," Laura said as the door closed. "Is she really the housekeeper?"

"She keeps house, which, dear Laura, is entirely

different," Cleo retorted. "It's said she was a singer in some third-rate opera company before old Zachary took up with her, but I don't imagine she was much good, judging by the bursts of song she treats us to . . . Perry says she hoped the old boy would eventually marry her after a decent interval when his wife died, but he never did, and she just stopped on and reared the kids, and now she's become a habit."

Poor Bella Spain, thought Laura compassionately, accepting the crumbs because they were better than nothing, and spoiling another woman's children for want of some of her own . . .

"Are there no servants?" she asked.

"Daily women from the quarry cottages — wives of the Zion workers, I believe, but Bella and Amos really run the house between them in an erratic sort of fashion."

"The person who was supposed to be responsible for the dogs?"

"Oh, those crummy dogs! Amos let them loose on purpose just to annoy Bella. He's a very rude old boy, a fire-eating chapel type who's been here for ever, and seems to do all the odd jobs about the place. He's convinced we're all earmarked for damnation and absolutely fascinates Nicky. Aren't children odd? Dom seems to scare him, but Amos's awful predictions and threats of hell-fire don't worry him at all."

"He probably thinks he's a sort of wizard or something. Nicky's a great boy for make-believe," said Laura with a reminiscent smile, and her cousin moved impatiently.

"Which you encourage," she said a little sharply.

"There's no harm in that at his age. He hardly ever has other children to play with," Laura replied, and her cousin said discontentedly:

"Well, do try to talk him round to a liking for Dom. I could cheerfully throttle the little beast when he turns sullen and awkward. He would have to pick on Perry, who couldn't care less but likes to score off Dom."

"You mean, he deliberately encourages the boy?"

"He doesn't even have to try — he's just Troy over again, and Troy could always manage Nicky."

"Oh, I see — well then, it's understandable."

"No, you don't see at all, Laura. There's more to it than manner and a physical likeness. They have certain traits in common which you wouldn't understand. Troy enjoyed taking away somebody else's toys, even if he didn't want them himself. It attracted me once — it still attracts me — but unfortunately it's Dominic who holds the purse-strings and it's *his* good graces that are important."

"I don't understand. Troy didn't take *you* from anyone, it was the other way about," Laura said, and Cleo made an irritable exclamation.

"Oh, be your age, darling! You don't know the half of that old story."

"But what else is there to know? Boy and girl elopements may be foolish, but they're hardly criminal."

"Well, I wasn't suggesting anything criminal! Anyway, forget it, it's dead and past, and who cares anyhow? Your job here is to guide my contrary child's thoughts in the right quarter. He listens to you, so start softening him up. You can try softening up the lordly head of the house too, if you like."

"I wouldn't dare," Laura giggled, and Cleo shot her a suspicious look.

"What on earth are you talking about?" she said impatiently. "He surely didn't make a pass on the way home from the station, did he?"

"Certainly not — in fact he warned me that the Trevaynes had no time for romantic fancies," said Laura with a fleeting smile, and shook the fine, mouse-coloured hair back. The gesture exposed the disarming nakedness of her curved forehead and lent her eyes the clear, untroubled look of childhood. For a moment her cousin saw her as she might appear to a man already sated with too many easy conquests and she said with a faint touch of malice:

"If I didn't know you better, darling, I'd say that sounds as if you'd tried a tentative pass on your own account. You really ought to do something about your hair, Laura — why don't you have a perm and go to town with one of these brightening rinses?"

"Your younger brother-in-law advised me not to be

tempted by rinses," Laura said sedately, and smiled again.

Cleo bounced off the bed with an angry flounce, and looked down at her cousin with a puzzled frown.

"I don't know what's got into you," she said crossly. "If my brand new brothers-in-law between them are already turning your head on such slight acquaintance, I tremble to think what the rest of your holiday will do to you."

"Forget it," said Laura with a disappointing failure to rise. "Your new in-laws have no part in my rather ordinary life, or I in theirs."

She could see by Cleo's puzzled frown that she had scored a point, but it gave her little satisfaction. She was already wondering what this come-by-chance introduction into affairs that were not really her concern might not do to her, but already since yesterday she seemed to have grown another skin, or perhaps, like Prince Lindworm in Nicky's favourite fairy-tale, she had shed one. She reached absently for her dressing-gown while she considered her position which, as she had just pointed out, could hardly matter to the household one way or the other; all the same she had an unquiet suspicion that life with the dark Trevaynes might demand protective covering; better to grow another skin than shed one and become vulnerable.

"You're day-dreaming again," Cleo said sharply, disliking her own unquiet speculations, and Laura sat down at the dressing-table and took up a hairbrush briskly.

"Quite right, I was," she said, "but if you'll leave me to get on quickly, I'll take Nicky off your hands for the rest of the morning."

Cleo turned at the door and blew her a perfunctory kiss, relieved that she must have imagined a change in the hitherto amenable little cousin who, after all, should only be grateful for an unexpected break in her rather dull routine.

"Do that," she said carelessly. "His room is the end one down the passage from yours. He's been grizzling ever since breakfast for his precious Moo-moo, so I wish you joy of him. Be seeing you . . ."

CHAPTER THREE

IN the broad light of day Penzion lost its first impression of strangeness, revealing itself as a house of bad architectural design with haphazard additions which owed little to beauty or convenience.

The house seemed empty of its inhabitants that Sunday morning, and it was the little boy who took her on a tour of inspection, running from room to room with whoops and shouts, delighted with the advantage that a week's prior residence had given him over her. She had found him in the room at the end of the passage and was surprised and pleased to discover it must once have been a nursery. The wallpaper and rocking-horse and an old painted toy cupboard with one door half off its hinges were clearly relics of an earlier generation, and Laura did not know why she should feel surprised by the knowledge that the Trevayne brothers must once have played there, unless, in her slight acquaintance with them, it seemed difficult to imagine the very adult and slightly forbidding head of the family playing anywhere. She would, if left to herself, have been content to linger there, indulging in her easily aroused day-dreams, but the boy, after his first excited greeting, was only anxious to do the honours of the house before some grown-up could deprive him of his importance.

"This is the tea-room . . . that's the day-room . . . here's the book-room, and there's the parlour, only no one ever uses it — aren't they funny names?" he said. "Ordinary people have drawing-rooms and dining-rooms and libraries, but at Penzion everything's different, and *nobody*--nobody in the wide world could have such a splendid hall as this, could they, Moo-moo?"

"I shouldn't think so," Laura laughed, remembering that only last night she herself had stood in this self-same place and been impressed, until Dominic had gently mocked her.

"You like Penzion, then?" she said, a little surprised that the child, usually so reserved in his reactions to new places and people, should, in one week, have accepted the strangeness of a house as big and unfamiliar as this.

"Of course. I belong here, Cleo says. I have pirate blood, too," he replied, frowning at her ignorance, and she felt a twinge of uneasiness. It was only right, she supposed, that Cleo should impress her son with his just claim to kinship with the Trevaynes, but it would be a mistake, she thought, to foster an assumption of rights so early in the relationship.

"Nicky, you mustn't take too much for granted—" she began gently, and realised at once that at five years old he could scarcely be expected to understand adult warnings. He did not, as usual, ask for an explanation, however, for he had hardly heard her, so intent was he on revealing to her the pride of his newly discovered treasures.

"And *this,* Moo-moo, is the wonderfulest thing of all," he said solemnly, pointing upwards to a bronze statuette which stood out of his reach on top of one of the glass-fronted cabinets which were filled with a motley collection of curios and flints and shells and pieces of quartz. "Do you know what it is?"

"No," said Laura obligingly. *"You* tell me."

"I didn't think you'd know. It's a *unimecorn,*" he announced triumphantly. "It's a magic. Bella *told* me. It's the beast of this house."

"How do you mean, the beast of this house?"

"The guardian beast, the family beast — *you* know — like the Queen has."

"Oh, you mean a coat of arms. I don't think the Trevaynes would have a unicorn as theirs. That's just a model."

"There's one here, too—look " The boy darted over to the fireplace where, sure enough, the rough outline of a horned head had been carved without much skill in the great slab of granite that formed the chimney piece.

Laura reached up to trace the outline with a curious finger and at the same moment the front door opened with a bang, letting in a gust of wind which

35

sent a puff of smoke from the fire into her face, and a familiar voice observed:

"Inspecting our adopted family emblem? How are you, Miss Laura Smith? I told you we would meet again."

Laura turned, her eyes smarting, to find Peregrine Trevayne grinning down at her with the remembered mockery, and her first feeling was one of indignation at the trick he had played on her.

"How do you do, Mr. Trevayne?" she replied with distant coolness. "What a pity you didn't make yourself known to me on the train. I must have bored you with a lot of information you already knew."

"On your high horse again, are you? I assure you I was anything but bored. I was getting the reverse side of the coin, you see, and comparing the two was—er—interesting," he retorted, and she was silent, trying to remember what she had told him that could conflict with her cousin's version of their relationship, for it had been clear from the elder Trevayne's unspoken misconception that Cleo would seem to have inadvertently misled them.

Nicky, however, whose attention had been caught by the mysterious allusion to a high horse, caused a diversion by running to his uncle and tugging him by the coat-tails.

"What's a high horse, Uncle Perry? Is it a unimecorn? Tell me," he demanded, and Peregrine ruffled the round black head with a careless hand.

"Certainly it's a unimecorn," he answered solemnly, "and a very high horse indeed which your Miss Smith likes to mount at times, because she thinks it makes her superior."

"She's Moo-moo, not Miss Smith," the boy corrected him politely, "and I shouldn't really think she could ride on a unimecorn, should you?"

"You never can tell. There's a legend about that fabled beast. I wonder if you know it, Moo-moo?" Peregrine said, and as she burst out laughing and dared him ever to address her by Nicky's not very flattering pet name, the front door opened again and Dominic came into the house with Cleo laughing beside him, her hands to her head as the wind blew the dark hair about her ears in wild and charming disorder.

"Are you alluding to our unicorn?" Dominic asked, shutting the door behind him.

She answered, "Nicky seems very taken with it. Is it really a family crest or something?"

Dominic smiled and glanced up at the model of the unicorn.

"No, just one of my father's whims. He found the model up there in some saleroom, I believe, and had one of the men from the quarry carve the other one over the fireplace. He didn't make a very good job of it, I'm afraid, but you'll find others in odd corners of the house."

"Why not adopt it as the family crest, if that's what your father wanted?" Cleo asked lazily, sliding an arm about her son and pressing him to her. Laura's smile was involuntary and wholly appreciative of her cousin's instinct for a charming picture, but Peregrine saw, and his own smile was not so guileless.

"You feel, Cleo, that a crest—or why not a coat of arms—would lend tone to the rough Trevaynes?" he asked innocently, and she shot him a quick, rather wary look.

"Why not?" she said lightly. "I don't mind betting, if the truth were known, that a good many such sops to snobbery are phoney."

But Dominic intervened just then.

"Lunch must be nearly ready," he said. "The boy had better run along to Bella."

Laura stood irresolutely, uncertain what was expected of her. She was here, after all, to take charge of Nicky, but no one had told her what the arrangement was for meals.

"Does Nicky feed with you, or do I—will he—should he have his meals in the nursery with me?" she asked and jumped at the sharpness in Dominic's voice as he replied:

"Certainly not. You are our guest and will naturally take your meals in the day-room. I personally have no objection to the boy joining us, but his mother says he's used to being alone with his nanny."

"Well, Laura *is* his stop-gap nanny for the time being. She won't mind, will you, darling?" said Cleo.

"But I should," Dominic snapped with an unmistakable touch of arrogance. "Bella will continue to see to the child as she has done for the past week. Now, Nicky, run along to Bella, like a good chap."

Nicky promptly screwed up his face and began to cry.

"Horrid old Uncle Dom. I hate you," he wailed, and Laura, who could have cheerfully slapped the child for his stubborn refusal to make friends with the one man whose tolerance, if not liking, was so essential to Cleo's hopes, took him quickly by the hand.

"Come along, Nicky," she coaxed. "I'll race you to the nursery."

"Bella is in the kitchen. Nicky knows his way," Dominic said. "Run along, Nicky, you don't need Laura to take you; she wants to get ready for lunch."

Much to Laura's surprise, the child obeyed, though he muttered something uncomplimentary as he passed his uncle, and ignored his mother's little parting coo.

"You see?" Cleo said to Dominic, making a small moue. "We're both in the dog-house, I'm afraid, but you mustn't blame Nicky too much; he's led the wrong sort of life for a little boy."

"Yes, he has, hasn't he?" Dominic replied, and his glance lingered on her for a reflective moment. There had been no rebuke in his voice, merely a hint of polite surprise, but Cleo let her charming, sulky mouth droop again and slipped a confiding hand through his arm.

"I know I've been a bad mother," she said. "Nicky was born so soon, and Troy, you see, never took parenthood very seriously. After he was killed—well, I was too shocked to care, I suppose. I shall only be grateful to you, Dom, if you can act as——as deputy father to Nicky while we're here, so don't think I shall resent interference. After all, we *did* call him Dominic after you, so that gives you special rights, doesn't it?"

They had both been drifting towards the day-room as she spoke, and Laura became aware that Peregrine was standing there looking after them with a very odd expression on his face, then he suddenly threw back his head and laughed immoderately.

"That," he said, "was a very pretty performance—a very pretty performance indeed, though I doubt if the wool is pulled over brother Dom's shrewd eyes."

"What on earth do you mean?" Laura exclaimed. "Nicky was called after his uncle, and Cleo was simply explaining. What's so funny about it?"

"Rebuke accepted, if not entirely digested," he mocked. "You don't seem to know your cousin very well."

"That's a very silly remark since you've only known her for one week."

"Ah, but a great deal can be learnt in one week. You'll be surprised how much I will have discovered about you, Miss Smith, by the end of a week."

"Well, really! You have the most colossal opinion of your own powers, haven't you? At least your brother doesn't assume on sight that he's got you taped!"

"Possibly he's more subtle and uses other methods," said Peregrine with a grin. "But don't be fooled, Miss Bread-and-Butter, by brother Dom's rather better manners. You may find, of the two of us, that I'm a very much easier person to live with."

"Very likely, if all you require is an admiring audience, but that hardly concerns me, does it?" retorted Laura, who was coming to the conclusion that neither brother would be very comfortable to live with.

"Well, it will concern you for the next few weeks unless you hand in your notice and up and leave us like all the other nannies," he jeered, and when she protested, with a child's temptation to argue, that he knew perfectly well she was never a nanny, he shrugged his broad shoulders and shook his head at her.

"That literal mind again," he sighed, and went away, whistling.

Looking back afterwards, Laura was grateful that her first day at Penzion happened to be a Sunday, for the explosive background to everyday life with which she was to become familiar was subdued to a Sabbath calm.

After lunch, when she had settled Nicky for his rest, Laura fetched a coat, wanting to explore outside the

39

house, and poked her head round the door of the tea-room with the vague notion that her host's permission should be asked, but only Cleo was there, stretched out again on a sofa, smoking in sleepy idleness, dropping ash into the open box of chocolates on her lap.

"Where's Dominic?" Laura asked.

"With his feet up in the book-room, I shouldn't wonder. Do you want him?"

"Only to ask if I may go and explore outside."

Cleo crammed another chocolate into her mouth and spoke with indistinct irritability:

"Really, Laura! What on earth do you want to ask permission for? You're not a child."

"I just thought perhaps it would be polite as I'm a guest."

"Then you'd better forget our correct Auntie Flo's hints on etiquette. The Trevaynes are scarcely a polite family in her outdated sense—in fact they're often damn rude, as you'll find out. Dom won't thank you for disturbing his forty winks for idiotic reasons. No one bothers with anyone else in this house, thank goodness."

"That makes us sound rather lacking in hospitality." Dominic's voice said from the doorway. "And you libel me, Cleo, if you accuse me of taking forty winks. I'm not in my dotage yet. I was having a quiet pipe."

Cleo smiled up at him cosily, proffering the chocolates which he refused with a smile, and settling herself more luxuriously among the cushions.

"No, Dom, you're just the right age," she said. "Thirty-five is neither too young to be without worldly experience, nor too old to change horses in midstream."

"Is that a riddle?"

"Not a very obscure one. I was only pointing out that a man of your age is still in his prime if he fancies a change from celibacy, whereas a woman of the same vintage is no longer considered young."

Laura felt slightly embarrassed at such frank manoeuvres before a third party and wondered if Cleo was serious, but Dominic merely raised expressive eyebrows.

"Surely, these days, no woman admits to being on

the shelf at thirty-odd? No woman admits her true age, anyway," he retorted with a hint of irony, and Cleo gave him one of her intimate and very feline looks.

"*I* don't mind admitting my age," she said. "I'm twenty-five—nearly twenty-six, if I'm honest, and aeons and aeons older than that in experience and men."

"Dear me!" he said mildly. "That sounds very portentous and, if I may say so, rather silly. Laura, were you going out?"

Laura jumped as he suddenly addressed her. She had been listening curiously to that odd exchange, and thought they had forgotten her.

"Yes, I was—that is—you won't m-mind if I poke about the grounds, will you?" she stammered a little nervously, and looked unhappy when he unexpectedly said he would go with her.

She could do no less than agree, but she had wanted to explore by herself and, like a child, felt cheated by the casual whim of a grown-up. She turned to make a small grimace of discomfort at her cousin, but finding that Cleo was regarding her with a very definite expression of disgust, she realised too late that she should have slipped away unnoticed while they were still talking.

She forgot her regrettable lack of tact, however, in the pleasure of fresh discovery, and almost forgot the restraining company of the unwanted dark stranger beside her.

Penzion itself had to Laura's unaccustomed eyes a harsh, unfinished air as though the house had been carelessly dumped on the cliffs and then been left to nature. The grass which did duty for surrounding lawns was coarse and bleached white with salt, and although stone paths and steps and terraces, white with seagull droppings, had been laid out to lend an air of formality, they only seemed to accentuate the lack of flowers. The boundary wall, though clearly built in a tidier age of bricks and mortar, was, thought Laura, a poor way of indicating privacy when trees would have been so much nicer.

"Actually, they would have looked rather drunk," Dominic said, amused by his young guest's naïve remarks. "Do you see how the few trees there are lean-

41

ing all one way? That's the way of the prevailing wind, and even in the summer they don't put out much leaf. My mother, I believe, tried to make some sort of a garden when she first came to Penzion, but we're not sheltered enough up here for flowers. Don't let our apparent barrenness put you off the Duchy, though. When spring comes I'll show you the flower gardens down in Merrynporth where things grow with tropical lushness, and even up here the gorse makes a brilliant show of colour and, later on, the heather."

He spoke, Laura thought, as if despite his apparent indifference to the niceties Cleo found important, he had a pride in his bleak inheritance and would not have changed it if he could for rich green acres and the gentle elegance of mellowed brick.

"We are still in the rough, with no frills to hand on to posterity," he said, as if divining her thoughts, "but in a generation or so, Penzion may acquire the mellowness of more gracious living."

"What do you mean, exactly?" she asked, puzzled by the use of a phrase so at odds with its more general usage, and he smiled with a trace of irony.

"I mean what you and your cousin presumably take for granted," he replied. "There's been no social life at Penzion since my mother died, and even when she was alive, few women visited. Our amusements are masculine pursuits, shooting, coursing, sailing and fishing, and the local pubs provide an evening's relaxation. If things should change and the Trevaynes breed daughters as well as sons, the pattern will alter."

What a strange conversation, Laura thought, wondering if the dark Trevayne was, perhaps, at last thinking of taking a wife to make these things possible, but almost at once he seemed to forget what was probably an uncharacteristic lapse into introspection, and became again the conventional small landowner pointing out local landmarks and objects of interest to the uninitiated. He had, she decided, because the habit was one of her own, been talking to himself as much as to her.

"Are you weighing me up and finding me wanting,

or am I simply walking too fast for you?" he asked, looking down at her with a quizzical expression.

"You have such long legs and the wind is rather strong," she replied, seizing on the proffered pretext which, judging by the deepening amusement which lifted one corner of his mouth in that strange little twist of derision, did not appear to deceive him.

"You don't as yet take us in your stride, as your cousin does, do you?" he said.

"I—hardly know you—and Cleo takes most things in her stride," she answered.

"So I imagine. One wouldn't suspect you shared the same blood."

"No, I suppose not—but there's usually one plain Jane in a family, isn't there?"

"One of a different make-up, yes—physical attributes aren't very important, after all."

"Aren't they?"

"No. You're thinking, I suppose, that Trevayne characteristics come out so strongly that you know where you are and don't need to look much further."

She had been thinking just that, but was conscious now of a possible lack of insight in herself.

"You—the Trevaynes—seem to follow a pattern," she said, stumbling after that preconceived impression which might or might not be wrong. "Was Cleo's husband like you?"

"Troilus? Your cousin, I imagine, has already given you her opinion of Troy." He spoke a little dryly and she had the impression that he was reluctant to speak of his dead brother, though he added briefly: "Oh, yes, he followed the pattern, too, but he was more like Peregrine than me, actually."

Laura supposed he meant that Troilus and Peregrine had been alike in temperament, since the resemblance in all three was too marked to be mistaken, then as he looked down to give her another of those quizzical, slightly disturbing glances which were beginning to trouble her, she realised for the first time that his eyes which, last night, had seemed as dark as his brother's, were blue and in the cold light of day gave him, momentarily, an entirely different look.

43

"It's time we made tracks for home," he said abruptly.

He left her at the gates to find her own way back to the house, and took a short cut himself across the bleached lawn to some undisclosed occupation awaiting him in the stableyard. He whistled as he went, and Laura recognised the same jaunty, rather tantalising little tune which his brother had been whistling that morning.

Sunday supper, she supposed, was no less dispiriting than the traditional affair of cold meat and salad to be found anywhere, but it was Laura's first introduction to the Trevayne's anti-social mealtime habits. Bella, trailing her stole in the food while she absently mopped up any remains left in the dishes, was to become as familiar as the silence which seemed tacitly agreed upon while they all bolted their food as if time would be wasted in talking. The brothers ignored one another and left the table when they had finished without waiting for anyone else, and when Cleo, catching her cousin's surprised expresson that first evening, giggled and had a sly dig at no one in particular on the subject of manners, Dominic's mild rejoinder managed to sound perfectly reasonable.

"There are chores to be done which won't wait on the leisure of protracted meals, as you've been here long enough to find out, Cleo," he said. "Your better brought-up cousin will have to get used to our eccentric behaviour, I'm afraid."

Laura thought she detected a trace of mockery in his allusion to her upbringing, for Cleo seldom missed an opportunity to poke fun at poor Auntie Flo, but the men soon disappeared to occupy themselves elsewhere. Cleo lounged back in her chair smoking, enjoying her cousin's evident desire to leave the table, but with no intention of making the first move herself.

"You won't find dessert and coffee and after-dinner drawing-room conversation here, my sweet," she said. "The men of the house are singularly uninterested in social pleasantries, as perhaps you've noticed."

"I'm not used to dessert and coffee and drawing-room conversation, so that won't trouble me," Laura replied. "There seems to be quite a library in that little room they call the book-room. I shall enjoy browsing."

"Then do your browsing when Dom's not about. That room's his own particular den and he won't thank you for trespassing," Cleo said sharply. "Brother Dom won't, by the same token, want you hanging round his neck asking naïve questions about family history, either," she added waspishly, annoyed by Laura's failure to oblige by even looking uncomfortable, but this time the shaft went home sufficiently to make her colour.

"I can't imagine what you're driving at. There's scarcely been time for more than the barest civilities between us," she replied.

"Well, you annexed him for half the afternoon when I'd planned to have a rather serious talk myself, and anyone could see when you came back that he'd been bored to tears," Cleo snapped with the sulky self-justification of a disappointed child, but the front door slammed at that moment, male voices laughed and joked in the hall, and restored to good humour at once, she made a small wry grimace of apology at Laura and hurried from the room to join the men.

"She's wasting her time. Unicorns are not for her," Bella observed with startling unexpectedness, and Laura blinked. Hadn't Peregrine made some oblique reference to fabulous beasts and legends?

"Unicorns?" she said, wrinkling her forehead, but Bella, she presumed, had merely been speaking her thoughts aloud, for she simply said: "What, dear?" as if she hadn't heard, and Laura, who had such lapses herself and sympathised, did not pursue the subject.

"Do you think I might go to bed early?" she enquired tentatively, uncertain whether she ought to offer to help Bella with the washing up since she had seen no sign of any servants all day, and jumped when Dominic spoke somewhat irritably from the doorway.

"For heaven's sake! You don't have to ask permission for everything you do in this house, as your cousin's already told you. You'll be enquiring next if you may take a bath!"

"Well, that's not so extraordinary in a strange house. Someone else might want one, or the water could be cold," Laura retorted, and he grinned.

"Yes, well . . . you clearly have the advantage over us of a nice upbringing," he said, and Bella eyed him with absent attention.

"I brought the two younger boys up with some of the good old-fashioned notions, I thought, but perhaps not—one forgets. You were too old in any case," she observed, and began piling up the dishes.

"Can I help?" asked Laura, reaching for a plate.

"No, you cannot," Dominic said before Bella could speak. "The dishes are left in the sink for the daily women in the morning, and Bella won't thank you for interfering. Get off to bed, and if you want that bath, go and have it."

"Well, goodnight," Laura said awkwardly, but since he was blocking the doorway, she could only stand politely before him waiting for him to move.

He was supporting himself idly with both hands pressed against the framework of the door. The bright knotted scarf at his throat was a little awry and his eyes looking down at her seemed in that uncertain light to be as black and bold as Peregrine's.

"I hadn't bargained for something like you thrown in for good measure when I invited my new relations to visit us," he said, and Laura did not much care for the inflection in his voice, that dark voice so different from his brother's. He seemed to be annoyed with her, and she wondered if perhaps Cleo had only spoken the truth when she said he had been bored with her.

"You expected a nanny, didn't you? Well, I'm simply here to look after Nicky, so don't let that trouble you," she said with a crispness born of the decision that she had at last had enough of the dark Trevaynes' curious sense of humour, but he shook his head at her, and now there was no mockery in his eyes, only a grave attention as his glance rested on her.

"Oh, no," he said. "You are first and foremost a guest in my house; the boy is a secondary consideration—do you understand?"

She shook her head dumbly, only understanding that

46

if, for some obscure reason, he was proposing to make trouble between herself and Cleo in order to assert his own supremacy, her visit here, looked on in the light of a holiday, would scarcely be without its difficulties.

"Never mind, you will," he told her with a faint smile. "You will have to get used to our ways, Miss Laura Smith, just as we, no doubt, will get used to yours. Your head's aching, isn't it?"

"A bit."

"Then get off to bed. You'll find, when you get to know us, the Trevayne bark is worse than its bite. Goodnight."

It was surprising, Laura thought in the days to come, how used one did get to things which were not normally calculated to reassure. Even the explosive altercations which blew up without warning between the brothers could be ignored, though not enjoyed. Laura, despite her inexperience in the matter of living, possessed the enviable gift of adapting herself to what came, and already the hostel and the flower shop and the daily trek to work and back seemed as unreal as the anticipation of this unlikely holiday had been.

"How lucky for me that Nicky's nanny decided to walk out," she said to her cousin, but Cleo eyed her with a certain amount of reserve.

"I'm not sure it was altogether a good idea," she replied. "You're so impressionable, Laura. It would be a pity if you began to get romantic notions about my colourful brothers-in-law. Perry's started in already, hasn't he?"

"What do you mean?"

"You know quite well. Perry can't keep his hands off any girl, however dumb she may appear. Besides, he likes to annoy Dom."

Laura was silent while she considered the implications. Peregrine's brash advances in idle moments had scarcely given her an exalted opinion of her own attractions, but she found him easier to get on with than the less calculable Dominic.

"Why should Peregrine's inability to resist flirtation

annoy his brother?" she asked. "Dominic hasn't any interest in me."

"No, darling, very obviously not," Cleo said with an amused little chuckle. "But Dom, for all his inherited Trevayne blood, has old-fashioned notions about hospitality, I suspect, and he knows Perry of old."

"It's scarcely any concern of his if I happen to prefer his brother," said Laura coldly, and Cleo yawned.

"Of course not, most women would, but it could rankle all the same, and Perry knows it," she said. "Besides, that was Troy's trick."

"What was?"

"Adding up scores, taking what he didn't want just for the hell of it."

"That doesn't sound very nice."

"He wasn't very nice, darling, in your meaning of the word—in fact he was no good, but he was fun and never, never dull, and Perry's too damn like him for comfort."

Cleo spoke with such sudden bitterness that Laura felt ashamed of her own impatience.

"If Peregrine so reminds you, wouldn't he—wouldn't he fill the gap?" she asked shyly, and her cousin's beautiful, sulky mouth twisted in rather contemptuous amusement.

"Do you think Perry's the marrying type, dear, sentimental Laura?"

Laura was silent, her thoughts leaping ahead to the possibility of other safeguards for the boy's future than financial settlements, then she said: "What did you really expect for Nicky when you brought him here?" and Cleo smiled.

"Well, there are more ways than one of killing a cat," she said, answering the thought rather than the question. "The thing is—which?"

"Which what?"

"Which brother, you clot! Or have you got an eye on one of them yourself?"

"Oh, really, Cleo! I've only just met them!"

But Cleo was determined to tease.

"Well, watch your step, darling," she said. "Have fun with Perry if you like, but don't be surprised if Big

Brother takes a dim view if he catches on. He has, I suspect, rather old-fashioned ideas about young girls living under his roof, and it would be a pity if he sent my temporary nanny packing for forgetting her place."

It was, of course, just Cleo's way of passing a dull half hour to talk provocative nonsense and proffer goads, Laura told herself, but she was uncomfortably reminded of the lighthearted warning later.

Peregrine had returned unexpectedly early from the quarry for lunch and catching Laura in an unguarded moment standing on a chair to reach for a book, snatched her off it and chased her through the house, desiring, so he improbably said, to demonstrate a new throw in judo he had learnt. She sped across the hall, laughing, and crying out in mock terror, and collided with Dominic coming in.

"Hey, steady on!" he said, catching her by the shoulder, "What are you running from in such a hurry, Miss Smith?"

"Peregrine!" she laughed, forgetting for the moment to be circumspect in the house of a stranger. "He was threatening to throw me to demonstrate—"

Her flushed face and disordered hair had brought a smile to his lips, but the smile froze as he rapped out sharply:

"Demonstrate what?"

"A—a new trick in judo, I think," she faltered, feeling he had caught her out in a rather undignified romp. Peregrine most inopportunely elected to appear at that moment in search of her and she found herself the unwilling cause of a scene.

"Keep your horseplay for the tap-room and your current barmaids in future," Dominic snapped, and his brother's expression of teasing devilment changed to one of temper.

"Running to brother Dom for protection, were you, Laura?" he flung at her nastily. "I hardly had designs on your virtue, my dear, or were you hoping?"

"Shut up and get out!" Dominic said, and Laura, seeking to divert the storm with feeble protests, fell silent, aware that they had both forgotten her in the bitter exchange of words that followed. Peregrine's

49

taunts and shouting were less deadly than his brother's icy, controlled anger, but both outbursts seemed altogether out of proportion.

Peregrine finally flung out of the house and the explosive noise of his sports car intimated that he had taken himself off to more congenial places for the rest of the day, and Dominic turned his attention to Laura before she could make her own escape.

"I must apologise for my brother's little exhibition," he said with such a sudden return to grave politeness that she gave a nervous giggle.

"You were as bad as each other in your different ways," she retorted, because embarrassed though she had been, she scarcely felt Peregrine merited the blame for a harmless romp; but she saw Dominic's black brows go up in sudden coolness and was immediately made aware of her impertinence.

"There are several things about us you can't be expected to understand, Laura, nor are they any concern of yours," he said. "But while you are under my roof I must ask you to remember—"

"My place?" she snapped, without thinking. "Cleo told me only this morning I shouldn't forget it."

The tight lines round his mouth relaxed and when he next spoke it was with gentle thoughtfulness.

"Did she indeed?" he said. "That wasn't what I was about to say, in point of fact, but I should be interested to know what your cousin imagines your place to be."

"It was only a joke," Laura answered, her little spurt of retaliation dying, "nannies and things like that, you know."

He stood fingering the scar with that unconscious habit he seemed to have in moments of stress and asked unexpectedly:

"Is Cleo paying you for taking charge of the boy?"

"No, of course not—we're cousins."

"Relatives are no less in need of wages than others, surely? You're a working girl, I understand."

"I earn my living, yes, but my aunt left me a tiny income, so I'm luckier than most—I'd never starve, and—well, I've never taken money from Cleo for baby-

50

sitting and things, and—and this is a sort of holiday for me, you see."

"How convenient for your cousin," he observed.

She sighed, abandoning the subject, and his smile became a little mocking, like his brother's.

"Do we seem a rough, hot-blooded lot to you, Laura?" he asked, and she looked at him doubtfully.

"I don't understand you very well, but hot blood is your legacy, I suppose."

"And that absolves us?"

"I don't know," she answered awkwardly. "I suppose it would depend. One can't blame everything on one's inheritance, can one?"

"No, Miss Mouse, one can't. Well, as long as you remember that, when you're dealing with brother Perry, he won't harm you. Perhaps you've more worldly knowledge than I'd thought."

"I can look after myself very well, thank you," she said, stung to retaliation by her own thoughts. "I'm twenty years old, know all the facts of life, and don't take everyone at face value!"

The familiar expression of amusement came back to his face, crinkling his eyes at the corners.

"Don't you now?" he said, and began to whistle softly. He broke off after only a bar or two, but she had recognised the tune.

"What *is* that?" she asked, teased by an elusive familiarity.

"Don't you know? It's a ditty you should mark, learn and digest with that misguided taste in smugglers you seem to have," he retorted, but did not explain further. "Well, I'm glad to hear you can look after yourself and you are acquainted with the facts of life, whatever they may be. You're very young, aren't you?"

"People," she said, exasperated, "always make that sound like a dirty accusation. I must give a very poor impression of femininity."

He put out a hand and touched her hair with un-characteristic familiarity, tucking a loose strand behind her ear in an odd little gesture of intimacy.

"Don't resent your youth," he said. "It's part of that charm you have such doubts about."

She looked up at him in surprise and her eyes widened under his own very blue regard.

"How surprising you are," she said shyly.

"Did you think my boastful brother had a monopoly of the Trevayne ways with women?" he retorted, and now the little derisive twist was back, pulling up the corner of his mouth as he smiled with the old, careless tolerance, for foolish remarks. "You'll get the measure of us in time, Miss Laura Smith, but be sure you don't gather too many misconceptions in the process. Now, make a start on enjoying this so-called holiday of yours. Tomorrow's the twenty-first of March, the first day of spring. I must make it my business, mustn't I, to show you that spring really does come to Penzion?"

CHAPTER FOUR

THE first day of spring . . . the words held a promise that had something of Nicky's simple magic.

Bella came in with the tray of early tea which she insisted on bringing up each morning and came to stand behind Laura at the window.

"See the young green thrusting through the brown of the heather?" she said, pointing. "That's the first bracken fronds starting to unfurl . . . Garden flowers don't do up here, but if you walk along the headland you'll find thrift and periwinkle and pimpernel, and a hundred varieties of wild things, like creeping jenny and the little rock plants—only you have to look for them."

Even as she spoke, Laura began to see with fresh vision, and wanted to get out of doors at once and explore for herself.

"Aren't there old Cornish customs for the first day of spring?" she asked pouring out the tea.

"There's the Spring Festival, but that comes in April or May, and isn't much observed now," Bella answered. "I always think it's such a pity when the old traditions die. The Hobby-Horse parade used to be one of the local sights, and in Zachary Trevayne's time the custom was still kept up here, with the men from the quarry making the parade, but Dominic let it lapse. He ought to marry, of course, and then the old customs might start again . . ."

"Old Mr. Trevayne must have have had a large streak of make-believe in him—all those odd things he collected in the hall to impress visitors, and parades and processions and things," Laura said, and Bella smiled.

"Yes, he was very like a child in some ways—with a child's stubborn refusal to admit his own mistakes, too, and a child's unreasoning spite," Bella said, and her smile faded. "Troy, of course, inherited the same quirks, so that breach was never healed. He was too proud, or possibly too vindictive, even to let his father know that he had a grandchild."

"Peregrine said that day in the train that old feuds held a family together—provided meat to get your teeth into when the fires were burning low. It sounded terribly primitive to me," said Laura.

"Peregrine likes to talk for effect. He and Troy both got that from their father, along with other traits. Dom has much more of his mother in him, but of course his early years were spent with her . . . I suppose that's why I spoilt the other two. Even Zachary was indulgent when it came to taking them into the business. Dom started at the bottom, you know, and it might have been better . . ." Bella broke off vaguely.

"Which was your favourite?" Laura asked, knowing it would not be Dominic.

"Oh, Perry, my dear, for I took him when his mother died, poor thing—but I fear I was unwise in giving in so much to both of them, or so Dom tells me now. They were so much younger than him, you see, and I had an affection for their father."

"Why did old Mr. Trevayne take such an exception to his son's marriage?" Laura asked. "I know he had his heart set on someone else, but that's surely no reason for such drastic measures in these days?"

"Well, dear child, Troy had already got the girl pregnant, and since she came of a family that was well known and respected round here, it was a slur on the Trevaynes when he refused to marry her," she said, sounding surprised that such things needed explaining, and Laura experienced a little shock of distaste. Such situations, she knew, were common enough, but she wondered how much Cleo had known when she made that runaway marriage.

"Yes, I see," she said a little helplessly. "That would explain a lot, of course."

"The whole affair was very awkward—very awkward indeed," Bella observed with the dispassionate consideration of someone to whom the story no longer mattered. "Dom, of course, didn't make things easier by offering marriage himself and being turned down."

"Dominic did that—just to save the family pride?"

Laura exclaimed, and Bella looked at her with mild surprise.

"Well, not entirely, dear child," she replied, making ineffectual snatches at one of the perpetually straying wisps of hair. "He was in love with the young woman —she was his girl in the first place, you see."

"Oh, no! Then the old father hadn't picked her for Troy at all?"

"Naturally not. Dom was the eldest son and his children the heirs. Hasn't your cousin told you that old story?"

"No—she thought Troy was being forced into a loveless marriage by a slightly crazy old man."

"Is that what Troy told her? Ah well, I suppose it's possible he did. He only charmed the girl away from Dom for spite in the first place, you know, just as Perry charms little Nicky now."

"But why—why do they like to play such cruel tricks?"

"Because, dear child, Dom is the eldest, and Zachary's will made unfair provision—also he's different. The pack tends to turn on the odd one out, you know."

Laura finished her tea and began to dress. This very different version of the old story had shocked her profoundly and she wondered uneasily how much Cleo had known of the truth.

"Why didn't they marry—Dom and the girl, I mean?" she asked. "It was pretty decent of him, don't you think, to offer to father another man's child?"

"Oh, yes," said Bella indifferently, as though that particular aspect of the affair was unremarkable. "The girl wouldn't have him, as I think I told you. The Cornish have a stubborn pride, you know, and she said she did not wish to save her face at Dom's expense, but really, I think, she wanted Troy and wouldn't settle for second-best."

"Second-best? Dominic's worth ten of his brothers!"

"Oh, yes, dear child, but unfortunately that's seldom sufficient to counteract pure animal charm, and then, of course, the fight settled things. Women tend to support the victor."

"What fight?" asked Laura, remembering the tension which had opened up so alarmingly between the brothers only yesterday, and which at the time had seemed so disproportionate.

"Well, Troy, you see, tried to brazen things out by denying the child was his and suggesting Dom was responsible, and Dom knocked him down, and it became a brawl . . . When Troy looked like getting the worst of it he managed to palm one of the sharp flints lying about and slashed Dom's cheek open, then kicked him half-conscious as he fell . . . The quarry workers turned on Troy then, and drove him out of the district. We never saw him again."

"What happened to the girl?" Laura asked, wondering how in such a sparse and scattered community such public indiscretions were lived down, but Bella was already picking up Laura's tray preparatory to departure for the kitchen and her eyes looked vague again.

"The girl? She miscarried, I believe, though I'm not very sure, for the family moved away from the district. Someone told me she had married after all, but Dom never mentions her, so perhaps it was only rumour, and that, as you know, dear child, is very unreliable."

"Who's unreliable?" demanded Cleo, bouncing into the room without knocking. She was still in her dressing-gown and obviously not in the best of tempers. "Aren't you ever coming to see to Nicky, Laura? He's driving me frantic with his demands to get up, while you and Bella are just gossiping."

"I should have thought, dear Cleo, that you could have dressed the child yourself for once," observed Bella, offering such an unexpected reproof that Cleo looked quite surprised.

"Yes, I suppose I could," she said, "but since Laura's here for that purpose, I don't see why she shouldn't earn her keep."

"You do not pay for her keep—or for your own," Bella said, quite without malice. She was simply stating another opinion.

"Really, Bella!" Cleo exclaimed, a little annoyed. "That wasn't very nice! Nicky and I are invited guests

56

and also part of the family. It's scarcely your place to criticise me, is it?"

"Fact, dear child, not criticism—not at all the same thing," Bella replied, quite unruffled. "It's the first day of spring, so you must expect some changes—even rites, perhaps. It's also Sunday, now I come to think of it, which explains why the boys are not at work. They'll be clamouring for their breakfast, so don't keep me any longer."

"Sometimes I think she's more than just eccentric," Cleo said as she disappeared. "Who were you tearing to shreds when I came in? Me?"

"You were never mentioned," Laura replied with perfect truth. She had no means of knowing what version of the scandal Cleo had heard from her husband, but neither had she any wish to discuss such ugly matters until her own balance was restored.

She sat down at the dressing-table to do her face, and Cleo hovering impatiently in the background said:

"Oh, do come on, for heaven's sake! Leave your face till you've seen to Nicky—he won't notice if your nose isn't powdered, and neither will anyone else, I imagine."

"Very likely, but my morale would suffer. My face, unlike yours, isn't at its best still wearing traces of yesterday's lipstick," said Laura, proceeding with unhurried calm to apply the few aids to beauty she afforded her face.

"What's eating you, Laura? You're not often bitchy," Cleo asked with honest curiosity.

"Was that being bitchy?" Laura enquired, innocently flicking a comb through her soft, fine hair, and silently deploring its trick of immediately falling back into a childish bob about her neck.

"Not really, I suppose, and I can't talk, can I?" Cleo said with the occasional engaging flash of honesty which could always melt her cousin. "You look very nice, darling, very nice and very *jeune fille,* if that's what you were after. Now, do come along and do your stuff. Be seeing you . . ."

Laura's early morning pleasure in the first day of

spring had been somewhat diminished by the time breakfast was over, but Dominic evidently had not forgotten his promise of yesterday.

"I thought we might take the car and show you the sights if it's fine," he said. "You haven't forgotten the date, have you?"

Laura's eagerness returned at once, coupled in the light of fresh knowledge with a desire to please him.

"No, of course not. I've been dying to get out of doors and look for all the things Bella pointed out from my window," she said, and Bella, as usual, cleaning up any remains left in the dishes, loth to let anything go into the kitchen that could be reasonably disposed of at the table, beamed vaguely on everyone and said she would take charge of Nicky.

"Well," Dominic said, "I thought we'd take the boy with us and picnic. I haven't really had much opportunity for getting to know my nephew as yet. Would you like that, Nicky?"

"No," said Nicky discouragingly, and Laura administered a half-hearted rebuke. Dominic was only to be commended, she knew, for making an effort to establish a working relationship between them, but it was not a propitious moment to force issues. The boy had started the day badly with a mood of perversity, and a long expedition would, she thought, put a strain on all of them.

"Your mother will come too," Dominic said kindly, refusing to take notice of rudeness, "and Moo-moo, of course. Wouldn't you like that?"

Peregrine, who had been lounging back in his chair, throwing scraps to Rowley, taking no part in the discussion but absorbing each reaction with enjoyment, winked across at Nicky and observed with a conspiratorial air:

"I think we'll all go—take two cars and do the thing properly. You could have come with me in that sports job you like so much, but if you'd rather stay at home I'll take someone else."

Laura supposed she ought to be grateful to Peregrine for adjusting the balance so neatly, but catching the momentary disappointment in Dominic's eyes, she felt an unreasonable resentment for his brother's effortless knack of saying the right thing at the right moment.

"Well then, that's settled," Dominic said, rising from the table. You'll come, won't you, Bella? You can detect the signs of spring for Laura better than I can. Perry, if you're taking the boy with you, you'd better put the hood up, the wind's still cold. Laura, if you'd go up and tell Cleo to be ready by eleven-thirty, that should give her plenty of time to dress."

Having issued his instructions with authoritative briskness, he left the room to start his routine Sunday morning chores of wood-chopping, yard-swilling and attention to the boilerhouse and light plant.

"Home life with a predatory overlord, eh, Laura?" said Peregrine, cocking an insolent eyebrow at her, but she was not prepared just then to laugh with him at his brother's expense.

"You talk a lot of nonsense and you like to show off," she said in much the same tones she used to Nicky, and he suddenly abandoned his lolling position in the chair and made a dive for her.

"You won't put me in my place, you know, with nursery tactics," he said and kissed her roughly. "Now scream and say how dare you! Why don't you?"

"Because," said Laura, shaken but undaunted, "that's exactly what you expect me to do. Your technique isn't very expert, if I may say so."

"You cheeky young devil!" he exclaimed, and kissed her again, this time with a little more care. It was only the sound of Dominic's voice in the hall which made him release her, and Laura, knowing her face to be flaming with that uncontrollable habit of blushing, turned quickly away as Dominic appeared in the doorway.

"Looking for me, Dom?" Peregrine asked, with unruffled composure.

"Yes. I want a hand with that door in the washhouse, it's off its hinges again," his brother replied, and turned on his heel and went, without glancing at Laura.

It was a day, she thought, going upstairs to acquaint Cleo of their plans, that augured badly, despite its early promise. Peregrine was evidently determined to be teasing and provocative. Nicky would become difficult and overtired, and Cleo herself showed no great enthusiasm for the expedition.

However, by half-past eleven they were assembled in the hall as directed, Cleo looking charming and aggressively feminine in tight green slacks and a small jacket which cunningly emphasised the curves of her hips. Nicky, Laura was relieved to see, now seemed elated in a well-behaved fashion at the prospect of a treat he was persuaded had been purely devised for him, and even Peregrine had shed his affectation of Sunday indolence and assumed a hearty, schoolboy air.

Only Dominic seemed slightly ill at ease as they piled into the two cars, as if, thought Laura, he was unused to family expeditions and the organised domesticity of picnics with their attendant drawbacks and doubtful pleasures.

"Have you never done this before?" she asked him as he tucked her into the back of his car next to Bella, and he gave her a wry glance of amusement.

"You're quick, aren't you!" he replied. "No, I can't say Penzion's very used to the more civilised country pursuits. Women, you see, don't stay here very often." He had, she remembered, made much the same statement that other Sunday on the headland.

"Then it's a good thing Cleo and I have come, isn't it?" she said with that bright little nursery air of encouragement that always amused Peregrine, and he smiled.

"A very good thing, Miss Smith," he agreed with suitable gravity, and slammed the door.

They would go by the cliff road over Zion Head to see the view from Ram Tor, Bella told her, pleased by the rare opportunity afforded her to turn tourist guide. She babbled on happily about hut-circles, Druid stones, wishing wells, and a host of other attractions, but, as it turned out, Laura saw none of these things.

Peregrine had shot ahead and was soon out of sight, demonstrating, for Nicky's delight and his own, the superior speed of his car to Dominic's, but they came upon him pulled up by the side of the road at an exposed spot not at all suited to picnicking in the teeth of a brisk March breeze, declaring he would go no further with a brat who threw up all over his car.

Cleo, remembering that the expedition had been arranged as a gesture of good will by Dominic to further better relationships, felt impelled to offer ineffectual maternal aid, but it was Laura who cleaned him up and who would have dealt, too, with Peregrine's car if Dominic had not pushed her aside and told his brother to do his own dirty work.

"If you hadn't been showing off, driving on your brakes and taking corners on two wheels, the boy probably wouldn't have been sick," he said, and Peregrine, though he turned sulky, obeyed him, but with no very kindly reception of Nicky's tearful apologies.

"Never mind, old man," Dominic said, observing the boy's crestfallen face. He offered a friendly hand and for an instant it seemed as if the child would respond, but Peregrine chose to crack a feeble joke to win him back, and the moment was lost.

"I vote we eat our grub and go home," he said, burying the last of the soiled newspapers under a gorse bush. "Why you had to think up such an unlikely refinement as a picnic in March, Dom, I can't imagine. For God's sake let's get it over with and get back to our normal Sunday sloth."

"There's nothing to stop you taking yourself off," Dominic replied, controlling his temper. "In fact it's a good idea. If you're going to behave like a spoilt child, we'll all be better off without you."

"In that case I'll stay—just to nark you," said Peregrine with insolent cheerfulness, and Laura, knowing how easily a quarrel could spring up out of nothing, said quickly:

"Let's have a picnic down there in that little hollow. The boulders will shelter us."

After that they all seemed able to relax more naturally. The picnic as such, thought Laura, could scarcely be called a happy start to Dominic's better relations with his nephew, but observing the efforts he made to gain the boy's confidence, she felt sorry that Peregrine had elected to be one of the party. He seemed to have forgotten his discontent for the moment, but to every tentative effort on his brother's part to establish some sort of contact with the child, he added a counter-attack of his own. Nicky, with the unerring instinct of children, very soon realised he had become an object of attention and began to show off, and Laura, remembering the unpropitious start of the day, felt that a scene was not very far off.

Nicky, missing his afternoon nap, soon began to grow fretful, and when Dominic suggested taking him on to the cliffs to watch for a possible passing ship, he declined rudely and retreated to Peregrine's side demanding unicorns, not ships.

"I thought you'd forgotten your unicorn," Laura said with some asperity, and then because it seemed better to pursue an uncontroversial subject as a diversion, she said to Peregrine: "Didn't you say there was some legend attached to unicorns?"

Peregrine's eyes held a glint of devilment.

"Oh, yes, there's a legend."

"Tell us, then—it will amuse Nicky."

"I doubt if Nicky would understand. What do you think, Dom? Shall I regale our impressionable Laura with that delectable story?"

"By all means, if you think the myth is worth telling," Dominic replied, and Cleo yawned.

"Laura's a sucker for dreary legends, but frankly they bore me," she said, and Peregrine, half closing his eyes, sent her a very pertinent look.

"You needn't listen, dear heart, for this one will have no meaning for you," he said. "Well now—unicorns. In olden times when knights were bold and fabulous beasts as common as cows or sheep, it was the great thing to hunt unicorn, for they were fierce and untameable and not to be caught by usual methods of the chase, so what do you think they did?" He had an arm round Nicky and addressed the question to him, but his eyes darted between Cleo and Laura with mischievous anticipation.

"What?" breathed Nicky.

"Well, when they wanted to catch a unicorn they put out a young virgin as bait—"

"What's a young virgin?"

"Don't interrupt. Anyway, that's what they did, and the first unicorn that came along just trotted up and trustfully lay down at the maiden's feet, and so he was caught. Simple, wasn't it?"

"So simple that there was probably another sort of catch," said Cleo with lazy amusement. "Your so-called virgin was most likely an experienced little piece who knew her way around."

"Oh, no, that wouldn't have worked at all," retorted Peregrine, and Nicky, cheated of an ending he could understand, said crossly:

"That's a silly story, Uncle Perry."

"Yes, it is, isn't it?" said Dominic with an unexpected touch of distaste, but just for a moment his eyes had held Laura's with an odd expression.

"Perhaps it might be a good thing if we all went home," he said on a weary note. "This hasn't been a very successful introduction to spring for you, has it, Laura? Nicky, stop making so much noise, there's a good chap. You're too big to cry like a baby."

"He's tired," said Laura placatingly, fearing a fresh outburst, but to her surprise and, she suspected, to Nicky's too, he stopped crying.

"You see?" said his uncle pleasantly. "You can be perfectly sensible if you want, can't you? Now, would you like to stretch your legs and come with me and see if we can spot that ship?"

The boy did not answer rudely this time, but he shook his head, looking scared, for he was afraid to go near the edge of the cliffs, and Bella closed her book and said that she would take him back to the car and put him to sleep on the back seat. He went with her willingly, and Dominic said a little wryly:

"I suppose one of us ought to have thought of that before. It would have saved a lot of unnecessary tiresomeness all round."

"Do you find him tiresome?" Laura asked a little anxiously. It was so important that the child should not antagonise his new relations.

"I find his aversion to me far more upsetting," he replied in an unfamiliar note of defeat, and Laura was troubled. She could understand Nicky's disquiet, for there were times when she felt the same thing herself, but this was not one of them. Left alone with Dominic, with the wind blowing between them and the sun seeming to turn warmer on her lifted face, she was suddenly at ease.

"Perhaps you try too hard," she said gently. "Children won't be forced."

"I wasn't aware that I was trying to force anything, but it's a little galling when Perry demonstrates so effortlessly that he has the knack I haven't," he replied.

"Peregrine likes to show off," she said uncomfortably. "Nicky probably subsconsciously recognises a kindred spirit."

"Very tactfully put, Miss Smith. But don't run away with the idea that brother Peregrine's effronteries can always be dismissed as schoolboy pranks. Perry's twenty-six, and has a very adult attitude towards the more sophisticated pleasures of life, as you may have discovered already."

He had spoken lightly, but his eyes were grave, and she felt herself coloring. He had, of course, been well aware of the significance of that little scene he had interrupted after breakfast, and she was not sure now whether he was warning her yet again, or simply intimating that he did not choose to be fooled by her airy dismissal of his brother's behaviour.

"I can look after myself, thank you," she replied, hoping that he would take the hint that her private affairs could be no concern of his, since this time he was not personally involved in emotional disturbances, but his eyes were suddenly amused.

"So you told me yesterday—and know the facts of life, too, you said. Very well, Miss Smith, the point is taken and I apologise if I have trodden on your corns," he said, and she sent him a swift, puzzled look from under her lashes.

"You're laughing at me," she said, then, in tones of such surprise that he actually did laugh.

"Yes, you rather absurd creature—I do laugh sometimes," he retorted. "I hope you don't, like Nicky, find me strange and a little alarming."

"Unimecorns—" she said for no good reason, and his eyebrows lifted, "—unicorns, I mean."

"Do I get the connection? The old legend evidently made an impression on you—good heavens, what a guilty blush! Were you, by any chance, confusing me with that fabulous beast?" He started to whistle that teasing tune that was beginning to become irritating, but she was saved a reply by the return of Cleo and Peregrine. He, however, with his usual disregard for the feelings of others, at once drew attention to her heightened colour.

"Well, well, well! Dom, you old fox, I believe you've been making hay while our backs were turned. We've been making a little hay of our own, haven't we, Cleo, my pretty?"

"Don't be more of an ass than you can help," his brother said quite mildly, but his eyes went to Cleo's face with a considering expression. Even to Laura, it was plain from her cousin's sleepy satisfied smile that Peregrine hadn't wasted his time, neither did she trouble to deny it, but her eyes met Dominic's with open invitation and she could not have suggested more plainly if she had spoken that her preference would have been for him.

When it came to arranging how they should travel for the return journey, Peregrine declined flatly to take Nicky again as passenger and looked boldly from one girl to the other.

"Which shall it be? Will you fight it out between you, or shall we toss for it?" he said, and Laura, turning her back on him, declared with unusual tartness that she, for one, was in no hurry to scramble for the privilege.

"You don't high-hat me, Miss Bread-and-butter—not after this morning's little skirmishings," he said, and picked her up with a swoop to carry her to his car.

"Put her down!" Dominic's voice, dark with anger, startled them all. "Do you hear, Peregrine? Put her down at once unless you want your ears pinned back."

Peregrine obeyed, not, thought Laura, out of any regard for his brother, but because he wanted his fists free. She stood unhappily between them, aware of how much alike they were in that moment, their hard faces naked with savagery, their clenched fists and the fluttering handkerchiefs at their throats lending them a vivid kinship with their buccaneering forebears.

"If you want a fight you can have one—but remember what happened last time," Peregrine sneered, and Laura saw the scar on Dominic's cheek begin to whiten under the dark skin.

"There are no flints around here, or have you other tricks like Troy's?" he said. For a moment his brother's eyes fell, and it was a sufficient acknowledgement of weakness to enable the older man to regain his control.

"I'm not brawling with you simply to teach you a lesson in manners," he said with weary contempt. "Your passenger's choice is hers alone, and you've already heard it. Get in, Laura."

As Laura scrambled into the car she heard Cleo say with her husky drawl:

"Well, that leaves me, Perry, my doughty knight. You shall let me drive your snorting charger and I'll show you a thing or two to make even your hair curl. I wasn't married to brother Troy for nothing—come on."

They were away down the road before Dominic had started his engine, Cleo at the wheel and demonstrating very ably that her boast was no idle one.

"If they end up in the ditch it will damn well serve them right," Dominic said with a savage jab at the accelerator, and for the first time Laura wondered if he could have more than a brotherly interest in Cleo.

She subsided into unhappy silence, the day spoilt. By the time they reached home, even the sky had clouded over and, with a rising wind and the first heavy drops of rain gathering ominous force, it looked as though they were in for one of those sudden Atlantic squalls. Spring, thought Laura, as she dashed to the house for shelter, was still very far from Penzion.

CHAPTER FIVE

WHEN Nicky was bathed and bedded down for the night, Laura went to her cousin's room to make the usual evening report.

"He's asleep," she said, wondering if it would be more tactful not to mention the unpleasantness of the expedition. "It was rather a long day for a five-year-old, really."

"He's a pest, and you're not being much help in establishing the right relations with his worthy Uncle Dom, but of course, you prefer Perry, don't you? So Nicky, of course, will follow the crowd."

Laura sighed. Cleo, she supposed, was naturally becoming anxious at the boy's continued aversion to his uncle, but it was useless trying to force a child to an affection it could not feel. Laura tried to explain this again, but Cleo appeared uninterested. She seemed moody and irritable, and although she had changed her slacks for a housecoat, she had got no further with her preparations for the evening but lay sprawled on her bed, smoking.

"You *do* prefer Perry, don't you?" she said, and Laura who had been going to ignore what she had taken to be a red herring, replied patiently:

"I find him easier, that's all. He's spoilt and a show-off, but I don't have to take him seriously."

"Well, so long as you remember that."

"But Cleo, you can't blame *me* for Nicky's devotion —it's Perry himself who never loses an opportunity to score."

"That wasn't what I meant at all. Perry's mine, do you hear?"

Laura was so astonished by such an unexpected reaction from the cousin who had always dismissed her as a child that she burst out laughing.

"I believe you're jealous!" she exclaimed, and Cleo flounced angrily on the bed.

"Why not? I'm not used to sharing favours," she snapped.

"Well!" said Laura. "I suppose I ought to feel flattered, but I can assure you I'd far sooner dispense with those sort of favours. It's just less trouble to put up with the odd pass or two and avoid a scene."

"But you find him attractive?"

"He has a sort of swashbuckling charm, I suppose, but I don't care for his rather spiteful methods of amusing himself."

"So it's Dom, really, is it? Oh, well, you're safe there."

"Dominic? Really, Cleo, why are you so determined that I'm bound to lose my head over one of your rather uncomfortable in-laws? I'm not given to imagining myself in love even if I do indulge in other day-dreams, and however willing Perry may be to make conquests, Dominic, I can assure you, would give me no such encouragement."

"No, I don't suppose he would. All the same—come here, Laura."

Laura walked round the bed and stood beside it, puzzled and a little uneasy at this sudden promotion to an equal footing, but Cleo's nervous irritability seemed to have left her, and she stretched out a lazy hand to give a tweak to Laura's dress.

"H'm . . . that dress isn't bad," she said. "It really does something for that absurd waist of yours . . . your hair's behaving better, too, and you're probably right to stand out against perms and brightening rinses . . . Perry may have something at that."

"What *are* you talking about?"

"Something he said to me this afternoon. I thought he was talking about himself when he said you were the sort to raise the protective instinct in a certain type of man, but of course he was thinking of Dom's uncharacteristic streak of chivalry, and he does keep a rather predatory eye on you, doesn't he, darling? Don't let it fool you, though—it's just a kink of feudalism—like the crazy old father's mania for his fusty collection in the hall. So don't lose your heart—or your head."

Laura was relieved. It was clear now that Cleo and Peregrine had quarrelled, as they so often did, and he had provoked her with unlikely hints and comparisons.

If Cleo had wilfully interpreted them in another way it could do little harm.

"Why do you suggest something phoney in a sense of chivalry? Dominic was ready once to shoulder Troy's liability in a pretty selfless gesture," she said, for that careless little dig at Dominic had troubled her.

Cleo looked up at her with a sleepy look of amusement.

"Oh, you've ferreted out the old scandal, have you? Well, there was nothing particularly chivalrous in offering to father your own child, was there?" she said.

A sudden gust of wind and rain lashing round the house made Laura shiver. "You can't believe that," she said with distaste. "Troy may have lied to you knowing he was safe, thousands of miles away in Australia, but everyone here knows the truth. Troy fought foul, too, using a flint when he was losing. Did you know that?"

"Yes, he left his mark to be remembered by, didn't he?" said Cleo lazily. "Did Dom tell you that? He would, of course, paint himself in a noble light."

"Certainly not. Bella told me. She thought I knew, naturally, since we're cousins."

"Bella? Well, Bella probably covers up now, since Troy's dead and Dom's head of the house. What does it matter, anyway?"

"I think the truth does matter, and what's more I don't think you do believe Troy's version—you knew him too well," Laura said with sudden shrewdness, and saw the little flicker of betrayal in her cousin's brilliant eyes.

"Well, perhaps I don't. But Dom doesn't run true to form, and that upsets my composite picture of the Trevaynes—when I'd got them all nicely worked out."

"Cleo, how much longer are we going to stay here?" Laura asked, for it suddenly seemed to her that the situation was less simple than it had first appeared, and the dark Trevayne, on whom the ultimate decision rested, seemed in no hurry to make up his mind.

"Until something's settled, of course. Dom will take his time, being what he is, and I'm in no hurry as long as Perry's around to relieve the boredom. Why? Are you panting to get back to daily-breading and your dreary hostel? You won't have another chance like this for easy living, free of expense—unless, of course, I settle here, when I would naturally invite you to stay."

"Settle at Penzion? With Peregrine, you mean?"

"Hardly with Perry, darling, unless he cuts loose on his own. I might have to settle for Dom who, after all, does own the place. I admit Perry's much more to my taste, but beggars can't be choosers, can they?"

"Could you really bring yourself to live in the same house married to one man and wanting the other?" asked Laura, to whom such a method of self-torment seemed unthinkable, and Cleo smiled with patient tolerance for the callow sentiments of youth.

"But if I was clever, darling, I could both have my cake and eat it as well, couldn't I?" she said. "Perry wouldn't raise objections—oh for heaven's sake, Laura, don't look so shocked! I was only talking for the sake of talking—you're so infuriatingly literal-minded! Yes?" she called out as someone banged loudly on the door.

"Hey, Cleo! Are you dressed yet?" Peregrine's voice called, and Cleo sat up, her lassitude forgotten.

"You can't come in—Laura's here," she called, giving, thought Laura, a rather odd reason for his non-admittance.

"Well, put on something warm—we're going on the razzle later, and it's a filthy night."

"Okay!" Cleo called back, and bouncing off the bed, caught Laura round the waist.

"Darling!" she said, with one of her rare demonstrations of a casual affection, "I'm sorry I was bitchy and talked all that nonsense. Forget it, will you? Perry and I had a blazing row on the way home and I nearly ditched his car because I was in such a temper at the things he was saying, but now—this was Troy's way—call you all the filthy things under the sun, and then take you out on a colossal binge? He's so like Troy that it's uncanny sometimes. We used to quarrel and call each other foul names just like this, and then make it up in bed in the only possible way."

"You're in love with Perry, aren't you?" Laura said,

but Cleo only laughed, her sloe eyes brilliant with excitement and an odd, animal passion.

"Love?" she mocked. "Well, perhaps it's the nearest I'll get, but who cares for the finer definitions? I'm a man's woman, and the Trevaynes are certainly all men, even the rather incalculable Dom. Clear out now while I finish making myself seductive."

Laura went away, feeling somewhat exhausted having been subjected to so many unaccustomed emotional moods in one day, and it did not at all surprise her that Peregrine should be lying in wait for her at the bottom of the stairs, for he, like Cleo, was presumably in that same heady state of anticipation. He jumped out on her from the shadows, holding her prisoner from behind, and she stood quite still.

"Don't scream!" he hissed with mock melodrama. "Big Brother's just across there in the book-room and in no tender humour after that dratted picnic. He interrupted some unfinished business between us this morning—remember?"

She had forgotten that it was only this morning that he had kissed her so violently, but she did not struggle now, remembering that this was what he expected and hoped for. She kept her eyes on the unicorn prancing in proud disdain on the top of the cabinet and said coolly:

"Haven't you showed off enough for one day?"

"O-*ho*!" laughed Peregrine, delighted, and Dominic's voice across the hall interrupted with deceptive mildness.

"Up to your old tricks again, Perry? Why don't you pick on someone your own size? Come in here, I want to talk to you. Laura, you'd be better empolyed in the nursery till supper's ready. The boy may be needing you."

Rather to Laura's surprise, Peregrine let her go without comment, and she turned tail and ran up the staircase.

Dominic closed the door of the book-room behind them and reached for a half-finished drink which stood on the desk.

"Help yourself. We might as well have this out in

comparative sociability," he said, gesturing towards the decanter.

Peregrine poured a stiff whisky, and propped himself against the desk, gazing moodily at the books which lined the walls and which none of them read. He never felt at ease in this room which by tacit consent had become his brother's study and office. He and Bella seldom used it, and Dominic's habit of retiring here in the evening to work had become an established custom.

"Perry—" Dominic was saying. "I don't want to rake up old sores or make any more bad blood between us, but you've got to differentiate between your waterfront floozies and guests staying in this house."

"Oh, come off it, Dom!" Peregrine blustered. "A bit of slap and tickle doesn't hurt anyone. The kid is probably grateful for a little attention—she's not the sort to attract the boys like honey."

"Fancying yourself as the answer to a maiden's prayer?" Dominic asked without much change of tone, but Peregrine knew the signs; the little pulse suddenly visible at the side of his mouth, the scar beginning to whiten as it had that afternoon. There were times when it didn't pay to drive the boss too hard.

"All right, all right," he said hastily. "So I act the goat at times; Bella's spoilt me as she spoilt Troy, and you've had all the responsibility and none of the fun— I've heard it all before and it's probably true. You should have married, Dom, then we'd have had a good woman keeping us up to scratch, the patter of tiny feet instead of a pack of mangy curs, and the neighbours would have called."

His brother smiled involuntarily and refilled his glass.

"Yes, I've been remiss," he said with faint irony. "Penzion needs a more civilized life, no doubt."

"And heirs," said Peregrine slyly. "But don't fret on that score; the old man was knocking on for sixty when he got spliced, so you've plenty of time. Besides, you've got Troy's brat to fall back on if you prefer to remain celibate."

"That's not the same."

"He's the same blood and the old man's only grandchild."

72

"Well, we'll leave that subject, if you don't mind. What were you saying to Laura?"

"Oh that? I was only teasing." Peregrine shrugged.

"Have I got to point out again that you're not dealing with the class of girl you're used to?" There was a sudden bite in Dominic's voice and his blue eyes were frosty. "I will not have you amusing yourself at that child's expense while she's under my roof—understand? She's not up to your weight, and still wet behind the ears."

"Arouses the protective instinct in you, does she? I was saying as much to Cleo this afternoon, and she didn't much like it," Peregrine said, his eyes brightening as he considered fresh possibilities for amusement. "I read somewhere that in a certain type of man, the protective instinct is the male essence, the springboard of sex, so to speak, and you, my dear Dom, have all the earmarks of custodian and overlord."

"For God's sake stop talking a load of half-baked claptrap picked up from the trick-cyclists!" Dominic snapped.

"All right, all right," said Peregrine again. "Don't let my babbling drive you to extremes out of mistaken chivalry as once before—your ewe lamb's in no danger from me, so long as the delectable widow's around. Now, there *is* a wench up to my weight, or even yours, and no one could call the fair Cleo wet behind the ears —o-*ho*! That's struck a spark, has it? Had you got a speculative eye on our glamorous sister-in-law yourself?"

He saw at once he had gone too far, as the warning signs appeared again in his brother's face.

"Yes, you've struck a spark, though I doubt it's the one you intended," Dominic said quite quietly. "I'm quite aware, in my rational moments, that it gives you a childish pleasure to see how far you can go with me, but it's time you grew up, Perry. Drinking and wenching around is all very well for cutting your teeth, but there are other things."

"Our dear old dad hardly stopped when he'd cut his teeth, judging by the family resemblances to be seen around in these parts," said Peregrine. "I'm only carrying on the tradition."

"Whatever excesses the old man indulged in outside Penzion, the business came first," Dominic said sharply.

"Meaning I don't pull my weight?"

"Well, you don't, do you? Troy had no personal pride in the quarry, and neither have you. It's just an easy living."

"Easy? Hard manual labour, sweat and dust and eternal blasting?"

"Scarcely an accurate picture, is it? Neither you nor Troy started at the bottom as I did. It might have been better if you had. The old man made a mistake. If you'd worked with the men as I did, you might have shared some of Dad's pride in the business. He had to work his way up and so did his father before him."

"So you inherited the family obsession along with the largest holdings by virtue of starting at the bottom!"

"Well, there's a certain measure of justice in that, I would have thought, though what virtue there is in the matter is simply the accident of being born the eldest. That's really what irks you, isn't it—that I hold the largest shares?"

Peregrine shrugged and looked sulky.

"Well, you own the ruddy joint, as well as Penzion —not even a partnership," he said, and Dominic replied with kindly patience:

"Well, let's face it, you wouldn't want the responsibility any more than Troy did. I pay you a reasonable salary and your shares pay good dividends. What more do you want?"

"Oh, belt up, Dom!" Peregrine exclaimed. "You know you enjoy cracking the whip. If you didn't you'd have bought me out."

The hardness returned to Dominic's face and he said shortly:

"I couldn't afford to at the time, as you well know. There were heavy death duties after Dad died, and we're only just recovering. Incidentally, I've paid your gambling debts a good few times, so why should you grouse?"

"Well, you could afford it now; Troy's share, after

all, was ploughed back into the business, so that should help. I wouldn't mind having a bash at Australia."

"Troy left a son," Dominic said, and his brother looked up quickly.

"So you *are* going to do something for the brat, are you?" he said. "That should brighten his mother's provocative eyes. Pity the little blighter hasn't taken to you."

"I'm not, I've come to the conclusion, a person who inspires great liking in the young," Dominic replied a little bitterly, and Cleo pushed open the door.

"This is where you've all got to, is it? I've been drinking all alone in the tea-room and feel quite woozy," she said, her eyes darting from one to the other of them with mischievous curiosity. "Who doesn't like you, Dom? Has my tiresome son been rude again, or has Laura been showing a reluctance for your company? When I met her just now, she said rather acidly she had been sent upstairs to her proper place in the nursery."

"Yes, well . . . perhaps I was a little abrupt," Dominic replied, and she pricked up her ears at the note of regret in his voice.

"Well then, you can make your peace, because here she is," she said cosily as she saw her cousin hesitating just outside the door. "Come in, darling. Dominic won't eat you, whatever he may have said to upset you. Say your party piece, Dom."

Laura came into the room, her eyes avoiding Dominic but otherwise quite composed. She gave a quick look at Peregrine, suspecting he had been on the mat for his foolish behaviour, and smiled at him uncertainly. Dominic thought she looked like a little girl silently condoling with another caught in the same misdemeanour, as he watched her, with her full skirt swinging as she walked sedately and a ribbon round her head holding back the soft fall of hair.

"There's only whisky in here, so let's go back to the other room and have a quick one before Bella calls us," he said, and Laura was relieved that he had ignored Cleo's proffered goad and taken no notice of her.

Supper was one of Bella's more haphazard efforts. Bella's cooking, Laura had already discovered, was either excellent or consisted on more forgetful occasions of a curious if interesting selection of offerings which might or might not go round the family. Tonight was one of them and gave Peregrine the excuse he wanted to leave the table.

"Come on," he said to Cleo, "we'll go and find a bite of something in Merrynporth. Any takers? Dom, you'll be working, I suppose. Laura?"

She did not want to make an unwanted third, knowing Cleo's expectations of the evening, but neither did she wish to be left alone with Dominic, who might or might not decide to shut himself up in the book-room as usual, but he was already getting up from the table with a murmured excuse to Bella, so she shook her head.

When they had all gone she became very conscious of the silence of the house and the fact that the day had been long and fraught with explosive interludes. She wished she had thought to slip into the book-room before Dominic and borrow something to read, but she would look in on Nicky instead because she liked to watch him sleeping, then go early to bed.

The door of the book-room was open as she crossed the hall and she paused to pet the old hound, Rowley, who shuffled up to her for attention. When she looked up again, Dominic was standing in the open doorway watching her.

"He's taken quite a shine to you, hasn't he?" he said. "Poor old dog—he probably craves for a bit of affection. Don't we all?"

"Do you?" she asked, sounding surprised.

"Oh, yes. They say what you've never had you don't miss, but it's not strictly true, do you think?"

"No, but you have to give as well as receive."

"Very true, Miss Prunes and Prisms. Some of us, though, have to be shown the way. Were you going to bed?"

"In a little while. I was going to the nursery first. I like watching children sleep," she replied, and was surprised when he asked if he might come up with her.

They stood together in the old nursery looking down at the sleeping child, and Laura, glancing at Dominic's grave profile, surprised a fleeting expression of pain.

"He's very like you all, isn't he?" she whispered, seeing again the early stamp of heritage in the sleeping face, the indisputable blood tie which must have marked Dominic's own features as he lay sleeping in this same nursery.

"He's like Troy," he answered, as if repudiating her unspoken comparison, and the boy stirred and flung up an arm. Dominic stepped back quickly for fear of frightening him should he wake, and Laura bent over him with reassuring murmurings, but her hands were careless tucking his arm back under the bedclothes and the child woke.

"Moo-moo!" he said in delighted discovery. Her presence in the middle of the night could, he knew, be turned to advantage in the matter of a story if he was cunning.

"Who's that?" he asked, catching sight of the tall figure standing back in the shadows.

"Your Uncle Dom come to say goodnight," said Laura firmly, and prayed for Dominic's sake that there would be no scene.

"Do you know that when I was a little boy I used to sleep in this very bed with a night-light just like you?" Dominic said with admirable quickness, and sat down on the bed.

"*Did* you?" said Nicky, his eyes growing round. He was either still half asleep, thought Laura, or too astonished by the thought that his uncle had once been a little boy to take his usual exception to the visitor.

"Yes," Dominic said, casually stroking back a disordered black lock. "That used to be my rocking-horse over there. I called him Conker."

"Did you ride him, Uncle Dom?" asked Nicky, and his awestruck tones of incredulity so voiced Laura's own preposterous mental picture of the very adult Dominic Trevayne riding a rocking-horse that she burst out laughing. Nicky promptly joined in, sharing a spendid joke that of course couldn't be true, and Dominic said with mild affront:

"What's so funny? I was a very skilful rider in those

days, let me tell you, young man, though I did rock myself into the washstand one day, I remember, and broke the best water-jug."

"*Did* you? And was your nanny cross?"

"I didn't have a nanny. My mother looked after me, and she wasn't often cross," Dominic told him gently, and the boy's face clouded.

"Cleo is. She gets angry if I break something," he said.

"Well, I expect she has cause sometimes. Have you always called her Cleo?"

"Oh yes. She says 'Mummy' sounds cissy and would date her."

"And do you know what that means?"

"No," Nicky said indifferently. "Will you tell me a story, Uncle Dom?"

"Well, now, I don't know that I'm a very good hand at stories. What about asking Moo-moo?"

"No, *you* tell me," the child insisted, and Laura gave him a little nod of encouragement.

He began a story, half legend, half fairy-tale, haltingly at first and a little self-conscious, but the boy's entranced eyes never left his face, and only at the end when sleep became too much for him to fight any longer could he bear to close them.

Dominic tucked him up, dropped a light kiss on his forehead and followed Laura softly from the room.

"You see?" she said, looking up at him with shining eyes. "That's a beginning. You had exactly the right touch with him, Dominic, and I was proud of you."

"How absurd and rather sweet you are," he said, but the tender amusement faded from his face as he added: "What I've gained tonight I shall lose tomorrow, I don't doubt. I haven't Perry's gift of sustaining popularity."

"That's a defeatist attitude," she told him severely, "and Peregrine only does it to annoy."

"Because he knows it teases! Oh yes, I'm well aware of that, but I didn't think you were."

"Didn't you, Dominic? I think you give me less credit than you should where your brother's concerned."

He looked down at her with a small, slightly worried frown.

"Perhaps I do," he said. "Laura, if I spoke sharply to you earlier this evening, I hope you didn't think—"

"I didn't think anything, Dominic," she said. "I'm—I'm just beginning to know you a little, I believe."

"Are you, Laura? Well, if I bite again, just give me a kick on the shins. Now I must go down and do some work. Goodnight."

Nicky, in the days that followed, came to a proud liking for Penzion itself, and listening to his childish boasts that this was his home for ever and ever, Laura experienced a pang on her own account. She could not altogether curb a strange, awakening affection in herself for the place which had at first seemed so alien.

March had already slipped into April, and for the first time she began to think distastefully of the florists and teashops, the hostels which had always seemed adequate with an illusion of home, the few friends who, like herself, had no roots but were content in the contemplation of marriage or careers to make them whole persons.

"Perhaps," she said aloud on one occasion when these thoughts struck her more forcibly than usual, "one can never be really a whole person as a single unit."

She had not entirely given way to the habit of talking to herself, for she had heard someone come out to the stable yard where she was sunning herself on the old mounting block, and thought it was Bella, but it was Dominic who answered.

"Have you discovered that truth so early?" he enquired, and sat down beside her.

"Hullo . . ." she said a little blankly. "You're back early, aren't you? I don't think lunch is nearly ready."

"I had to go over the other side of the moor on some business and didn't think it was worthwhile going back to the works till after lunch," he said. "Why do you so often seem uneasy with me, Laura?"

She picked at a bit of moss, avoiding his eyes.

"I don't know," she said, too direct to try and evade the question with polite denials, and he smiled.

"Perhaps you share Nicky's distrust," he said, and she looked up quickly.

"Oh, no! I would trust you with my life," she said absurdly, and a faint twinkle appeared in his very blue eyes.

"Would you, now? That's very encouraging," he said with appropriate gravity, and she laughed.

"That was an awfully silly reply to make, wasn't it? Like the heroine in an old-fashioned novel," she said a little ruefully. "And Nicky doesn't distrust you, you know. He's just not old enough to distinguish between worth and—and glitter."

"What a very odd thing to say. One must take it from that, one presumes, that you *are* old enough!"

"Oh, yes. My Auntie Flo was a spinster and not very young, but she had a quite definite set of values."

"Had she indeed?"

"Yes, she had. That—" said Laura, eyeing him rather warily "—is the answer to your question, if you want to know."

"What, for heaven's sake! Which question? And how the hell does your Auntie Flo come into it?"

"She doesn't. It was the way you answered—the way you so often talk to me—rather as if I were Nicky. That's what makes me uneasy, sometimes."

"Oh, I see. You shouldn't, you know, take everything at face value—I think I've told you that before. One puts up such defences as seem proper."

"Defences—against me?"

"Well, you see, I'm not very used to young women stopping under my roof, so I'm probably not good at small talk."

"You don't talk to Cleo as if she was slightly half-witted," said Laura, refusing to be sidetracked, and he put a hand over one of hers.

"Cleo doesn't need handling with kid gloves," he said ambiguously, "but I'm sorry if I've made you feel half-witted. You do, at times, test one's ingenuity rather severely."

"Do I?"

"Yes, you do. You are such a mixture of common sense and highly astonishing absurdity that you must forgive a certain amount of confusion in the mere male."

She smiled, dimly recognising that confusion wasn't necessarily confined to the very young, and the thought gave her fresh confidence in herself. His hand still rested over hers and she felt again the hard roughness which would always be a legacy from those early days in the quarry.

"I wonder what you meant by that very profound remark I overheard just now," he said, removing his hand and thrusting it under his other arm, hugging his chest.

"About being a whole person? I suppose I meant that the perfect whole must be a shared one. To be a single entity is unfinished," she said, and his smile was a little crooked as the scar puckered up a corner of his mouth.

"One and One and all alone? I'm not, I think, a person who easily inspires affection."

"Dominic," she said on impulse, "—you mustn't let a—an old passion spoil the whole of your life."

"'I am desolate and sick of an old passion,' you were suggesting, since we might as well go on quoting verse," he said, and she saw at once the impulse had been merely an impertinence. "So you've got hold of that old scandal, have you? I wonder which version you've heard—not that it's of any consequence. I assure you I am neither sick, nor particularly desolate, and I'd advise you, my dear Miss Mouse, to keep your well-meaning little nose out of affairs that don't concern you until such time as might become fit for you to be told."

She sat there with her face aflame, aghast at her own temerity, and dumb with the agonised dumbness of shame. She had trespassed unforgivably without even the excuse of long acquaintance, and his cool withdrawal was like a slap of distaste. Although his smile was quite kindly as he got to his feet, he was, thought the mortified Laura, very much the arrogant dark Trevayne as he left her and walked away.

She avoided him after that, acutely conscious of having fallen into the trap of her own well-meaning clumsiness. It was, she thought, so difficult to judge another person's moment of truth, to know when it matched with yours.

"He is two different people, and I get confused," she said to Bella once, because with Bella one could sometimes speak one's thoughts and not be misunderstood.

"We all," said Bella, "build up our own defences, but we rarely understand the defences of others. Are you troubled about something, dear child?"

"No, that's not what I mean," replied Laura, wondering if Bella in her roundabout fashion was dropping words of warning as Cleo had.

"No. Very likely you are still only concerned for the little boy. What does your cousin hope for him?"

"Don't you think Nicky has a certain claim to Trevayne generosity?" Laura said gently. "It was Cleo's money that kept them all in the end, you know."

"Very likely," said Bella absently, and her strange eyes took on their psychic look as she paused in her task of laying the table and gazed into space. "Troy's child . . . he would doubtless have been provided for had Zachary known . . . he wanted a grandson to carry on . . . the next generation . . ."

"Well, Nicky is the next generation and the only one left, isn't he?" Laura said, becoming impatient at so much beating about the bush over something which to her seemed simple and straightforward.

Bella did not answer, but her eyes lost their fixed stare and travelled over Laura's shoulder to the open door, so it was no surprise when Dominic's voice spoke behind her:

"If you're pleading your cousin's cause, Laura, it would be better to take the matter up with me," he said, and she turned away to hide her hot cheeks.

"I wasn't pleading any cause, unless, perhaps, Nicky's," she answered, embarrassed but prepared to stand her ground. "I was only pointing out to Bella that he carries your name and your blood and is, after all, the last of your line."

"Very grandiloquently said, Miss Mouse, but possibly premature," he replied with gentle irony. "I may marry."

"Oh!" she exclaimed.

"You hadn't thought of that, had you?" he said. She could not tell him that she had certainly thought, but been misled by his own attitude.

"Well, of course—I mean—" she stammered, and he grinned at her rather unkindly.

"I don't think you know what you mean, and perhaps it's just as well," he said. "Did your cousin put you up to this?"

She looked round anxiously for support from Bella, but Bella had gone.

"Well?" said Dominic, a faintly ominous note coming into his voice, and Laura turned and looked him straight in the eye.

"Cleo put me up to nothing. She's quite capable of pleading her own cause," she retorted, and the corners of his mouth twitched slightly.

"So I would imagine. You, however, have a remarkable gift for interference," he replied, and she moved too hastily and knocked over a salt-cellar.

"*Now* look what you've done!" she exclaimed, thankful for the diversion, but childishly dismayed by the significance of spilled salt between them.

"I didn't do it," he protested mildly, and she missed the faint twinkle in his eye. "Are you superstitious, Laura?"

"Yes . . . oh, yes . . . walking under ladders, broken mirrors, black cats, spilling salt—all terrible bringers of bad luck," she said somewhat incoherently, and threw a handful of salt over her left shoulder. "You'd better do the same, Dominic, or we shall quarrel."

"You have a rather engaging method of sidetracking a subject," he observed. "Do I make you nervous?"

"No—yes—oh, *do* throw some salt over your left shoulder or we really *will* quarrel."

He obliged with a small mocking snap of finger and thumb, finishing up with an admonitory flip to her cheek.

"If we ever do quarrel, Miss Mouse, you won't be left in any doubt," he said, and sauntered out of the room.

CHAPTER SIX

HE returned to the subject most unexpectedly that same evening, however. Cleo and Peregrine had gone racing, to finish up, doubtless, with one of their pub crawls, and Laura found herself committed to a solitary evening with Dominic. Bella left the table halfway through supper and did not return, and Laura, used by now to the abrupt departures of the household upon finishing their meals, expected Dominic to do the same, but he sat on, pushing his chair back to relax and watch her efforts to catch up.

"You'll choke," he said. "Where's the hurry?"

"You all eat so fast, I'm always left behind," she complained. "Don't wait for me, Dominic, you never do."

"Yes, I'm afraid we're somewhat lacking in table manners. No woman around to make polite small talk, I suppose. Bella doesn't count. Do you dislike being watched eating?"

"Yes, it makes me nervous."

"I make you nervous, too, upon occasion, I suspect?"

"Yes, sometimes."

"And Perry doesn't?"

"Not in the same way. I can be rude to him, you see, and that puts us on the same level."

"Does it indeed? And you feel, I gather, you can't be rude to me. Is it my great age?"

"Of course not. You surely don't consider thirty-five or thirty-six old?"

"Well, perhaps not. All the same, there's fifteen years' difference between us."

"Between us? Well, does it matter?"

"It might," he said, and she stopped eating and sat looking at him with puzzled uncertainty.

"It isn't," she said at last, "anything to do with age."

"What isn't?"

"Feeling nervous. You're tying me up, Dominic."

He smiled then with Peregrine's familiar teasing

mockery, and she reflected that ten years ago he must have been very like his brother.

"I'm sure," she said uneasily, "you must have things to do. You don't sit about much in the evenings."

"Well, this is going to be an exception, so it's no use trying to get rid of me. I want to talk to you, so hurry up and finish your pudding," he said, and she took up her fork again and bolted the rest of her food in silence.

"Finished?" Dominic asked abruptly, and without waiting for a reply, pushed back his chair and went to the door.

"I think I should go up and see that Nicky's all right," she said hurriedly, and then wished she hadn't spoken when she saw his grin of amusement.

"A lame excuse, Miss Mouse, and one you seem fond of. The boy was asleep hours ago, as you very well know. Are you afraid I'm going to eat you?" he said, and she was glad of the dimness as she felt her cheeks grow hot. Was he imagining she thought he had designs on her?

"Certainly not!" she retorted, taking refuge in the reprimanding tones she sometimes used to Nicky, and his grin grew broader.

"You won't put *me* in my place with your prunes and prisms," he said rather unkindly, and went into the book-room, leaving the door open for her.

The room with its book-lined walls and tapestry hangings, was more friendly by night, she thought, her eyes beginning to rove over book titles, picking out old favourites. One desk-lamp and the firelight lent an illusion of cosiness that the rest of the house lacked, and she forgot her uneasiness.

She sat down on a low stool by the fire and waited expectantly, and the old hound who had followed them in lay down beside her.

"What do you want to know?" she asked as he did not at once speak. "You can see for yourself that he's quite a well-behaved little boy, considering he's so much with grown-ups, and in time—in time he'll lose that—that reserve he has with you."

"Very delicately put," he replied a little dryly, sitting down behind the big desk and reaching for a pipe. "His reserve, as you call it, is plain dislike I'm afraid, but that can't be helped. What, in your opinion, do you consider I should do about him?"

"Me?" She sounded surprised. "Financially, you mean?"

"Oh, financially, of course—that was the main object of the visit, wasn't it? But there are other considerations. You seemed very ready to express your views to Bella. I'd like to hear them."

"But my views can't matter, it's Cleo's affair. You must have discussed things with her."

"As a matter of fact, I haven't, but that doesn't mean I haven't done some serious thinking."

"Oh!" Laura sounded as nonplussed as she felt, and he gave her a little smile of encouragement.

"Come now, Laura, it was you who pointed out only this morning that my family had a duty to Troy's son— the last of our line, I believe you said."

She was not very sure whether he wasn't still mildly rebuking her for interference, but he seemed to expect an answer.

"Well, don't you think you have—a duty, I mean?" she replied. He had, after all, invited her opinion.

"Oh, certainly. I never shared my father's stubborn attitude, and tried, as I think you know, to contact my brother after the old man died, but Troy was as head-strong and revengeful as his father. It might have made a difference, you know, if the news of a grandson hadn't been kept from us."

"But that, surely, could have been pride on Troy's part."

"It was spite as well, my dear. The old man cared more about being cheated out of a grandchild than he cared about Troy marrying your cousin."

"Yes, I see . . . I don't, you must understand, know very much about those years in Australia. Cleo came home every once in a while and dumped Nicky on my aunt while she paid visits, but I was still at school and Cleo seldom wrote . . . They were always moving about, and I think money was short . . ."

"I see. Well now, what would you consider my ob-ligations to be?"

She was so long in replying that he tilted the lamp at his elbow to shine it more fully on her face. She looked like a little girl, he thought, sitting on the stool with her feet together, twisting her hands in her lap, and his smile was suddenly tender as he watched her.

"I don't know how to answer you, Dominic," she said at last. "I—I think you should be responsible within reason for Nicky's future, since your brother no longer can be, and it's hard on a young widow to bring up a boy alone."

"Your cousin is far too decorative to remain a widow long," he said with a certain crispness, and Laura gave him a quick look, wondering whether there was any deeper significance in that remark.

"But a child can be a handicap to a second marriage," she pointed out gently. "Cleo knows only too well that a boy needs a father, but another man's child can be an added financial responsibility these days."

"I see. So you think a settlement would clear the way for remarriage?"

"Well, it would help to make her independent of another man's generosity, wouldn't it?"

"You've got it all nicely worked out between you, haven't you?" he said, and spoke with such unexpected harshness that she jumped. He had jerked his chair round abruptly and the light from the desk-lamp now fell full on his face, cruelly exposing the puckered scar. As if he were aware of it he put a hand to his cheek with that automatic, defensive little gesture which had become familiar, and Laura said, her first recoil at his sudden change of manner forgotten in swift compassion:

"Forget your scar, Dominic—no one notices it but you."

"And the boy," he retorted, but he dropped his hand to his knee with the sheepish haste of someone caught out in an unconscious habit of betrayal and pushed his chair back out of the light.

"It scared him a little at first, perhaps, but children accept physical differences very quickly. Nicky thinks you're a pirate and another pirate attacked you with a cutlass."

His laugh was spontaneous, and held both relief and amusement.

"And I suppose *you* invented that one for him! Oh, Laura, my solemn child, sometimes I think you enjoy your fantasies as much as Nicky does. Penzion will seem a duller place when you've gone."

"Will it?" she said politely, but she looked suddenly blank. Their visit had lengthened so imperceptibly that thoughts of the morrow had been pushed aside, but she knew it must end once Cleo's affairs were straightened out, and she knew now that she did not want to go.

"You sound sceptical. Don't you think you will be missed?" he asked, and she leaned forward, trying to see his face in the shadows.

"I hadn't thought about it," she said. "I was a—a sort of gatecrasher really, I suppose, and it's I who will miss Penzion."

"Laura," he said suddenly, "I'd like to bring the boy up here. Does that sound feasible to you?"

Her eyes widened in surprise.

"It would be wonderful for Nicky, of course, he loves Penzion, but—but how could you arrange that? Did you mean adoption?"

"Well, no—he already has a parent. But there are other ways—other considerations. I just wanted to get your reaction."

She sat silent while she considered those unnamed possibilities. Marriage? And if so, marriage of course with the boy's mother . . . by what other means could one gain control of a child? She felt suddenly drained.

"You've already made your plans, of course," she said, wondering why she should have imagined he had a use for her opinions. The Trevaynes, from what she knew of them, were not the sort to seek counsel pending their decision.

"Oh, yes, I've made my plans—and my conditions," he said, still watching her.

"Then you'll act on them, won't you? And your affairs are really no concern of mine," she said gently, and thought he looked disappointed.

"I think I'll go to bed if you don't mind," she said, and he bade her an absent goodnight and made no effort to detain her. He saw her, however, reach up a hand to the shelves to finger the leather binding of a book as she passed on her way to the door, and added:

"You're fond of books, aren't you? Yes, of course you are—all those odd quotations and jingles. Use the room when you like and borrow what you want."

"Thank you," she said. "I'll stick to the day-time so I won't be in your way."

She had the door open now, but before she could make her escape, the front door was flung wide and Cleo and Peregrine entered noisily. Cleo seeing Laura in the lighted doorway of the book-room moved quickly across the hall.

"Dom still up?" she asked, pushing past. "Oh, you are. We've had a fabulous evening—all those funny little waterside taverns, and sailors with rings in their ears, and the local floozie practically doing a strip-tease! Laura should have been with us—her eyes would have popped out on stalks, Perry, we must take my credulous little cousin with us some time," she added as Peregrine joined them.

Dominic had risen and he spoke now with a certain sharpness.

"You'll not take Laura to your sleazy joints—understand, Perry?"

Peregrine grinned and gave Cleo a significant wink, to which she returned a grimace.

"Hardly sleazy, Dom—just picturesque local colour, as you should know. Is my little cousin so innocent that she must be protected from the rougher side of life, or am I so hardboiled that it doesn't matter?" she asked, and surveyed him with provocative good humour.

"You," Dominic replied, "are of the same stuff as the Trevaynes. Our rougher side of life would hardly dismay you."

Although he spoke harshly, he made it sound like a compliment, and Cleo clearly took it as such, for she slanted her eyes at him provocatively and said, "Of course not, I belong. I do belong, don't I?"

If it was a deliberate challenge, Dominic met it with blandness, though his eyes were bright with speculation.

"Oh, yes, you belong," he said, and Peregrine, whose

dark eyes had been going from one to the other of them with a hint of sullen annoyance, observed:

"Well, you don't seem to have wasted your time either, dear brother. Was our obliging Laura helping with the office work, or were you merely keeping company? The book-room is debarred to most of us."

He was, Laura realised, a little the worse for drink, and she trusted that he was not going to come out with one of his more embarrassing effronteries.

"I was going to bed," she said, hoping to divert him, but although he obligingly offered no tiresome jibe, Cleo's attention was caught.

"Well, what d'you know?" she said silkily. "Little Laura, all starry-eyed from an evening with the bas! Have we come back at an inopportune moment, darling?"

She, like Peregrine, Laura saw, had had enough to make her careless, but Dominic, apparently, was more amused than annoyed.

"Your cousin, I think, is hardly impressed with the honour done her," he said. "She was in a hurry to retire, as she told you. Would you like a nightcap, Cleo?"

"Why not?" said Cleo cosily, sinking on to Laura's stool. "Oh, are you going, Laura?"

She scarcely had much choice, thought Laura crossly, slipping through the doorway. She did not wish to remain, listening to their familiar wrangles, but neither did she care for being dismissed like an importunate child.

Peregrine, who had slipped out after her, caught her in the shadows.

"Disappointed in brother Dom's technique?" he asked, turning up her face. "You should be content with me, Miss Bread-and-butter—at least I know what satisfies little girls."

She had no chance of avoiding his kisses, but, unlike other occasions, she found herself responding, not because he had any great attraction for her, but because for the first time in her life she was curious and felt a desire to experiment.

"Well . . ." he said as he released her, "do I detect

a change of heart, or has brother Dom been giving you lessons?"

"Your brother," she retorted, her cheeks flaming, "is hardly likely to make love to pass the time, as you should know. Now, please let me go to bed."

"Disappointed, evidently," he remarked unkindly, and fell to whistling that maddening little tune as he went back to the book-room, and Laura knew it was true.

She went unhappily to bed and lay there in the darkness, probing her own emotions. Day-dreams were all very well if kept in their proper places; it had done no harm to weave colourful fantasies about the dark Trevaynes and their buccaneering forebears, but it wouldn't to to lose one's heart to one of them—it wouldn't do at all. . . .

The next day the brothers had gone to work long before Laura could be embarrassed by the presence of either, but Cleo was curious.

"What went on between you and Dom last night?" she asked when Laura brought up her breakfast. "You don't usually pursue him to his lair."

"Nothing," Laura answered sedately. "He wanted to talk about Nicky, as a matter of fact."

Cleo became immediately alert.

"What did he say? What did you gather?" she asked eagerly, and Laura looked at her curiously.

"Why haven't you discussed things with him yourself?" she asked, and Cleo looked smug.

"Because, darling, I'm a sensible girl and know my onions. So much better, don't you think, if suggestions come from him?"

"Yes, I suppose so. I think he's made up his mind."

"And discussed it with you? Well, what's the verdict?" Cleo asked, and Laura wandered over to the window, as she did each morning now April had come, to look for the signs of spring that Bella had taught her. She wished that she could stay for summer and watch the rich fulfilment of the land.

"Laura! You're day-dreaming again! What did you get out of Dom?" said Cleo's impatient voice behind her, and she turned back to the bed.

"He wants to bring Nicky up here," she said colourlessly, and Cleo stretched and yawned.

"Does he now? How very cosy! And how, did you gather, does he propose to set about that?"

"I don't know. He just said he had made certain plans and there were conditions."

"Conditions? But didn't you ask him for chapter and verse? Really, Laura, sometimes I think you do it on purpose!"

"Do what? It was hardly my place to ask for explanations—that must be between the two of you. Conditions *could,* of course, refer to legal aspects."

"Is that what you really think? No, of course you don't! The poor dear was probably angling for a line on what my reactions would be Didn't you throw out a cousinly hint that I might be interested?"

"We only discussed it generally—in fact—"

"In fact the whole thing was an excuse on Dom's part for a little cosy get-together, I'm beginning to think," said Cleo petulantly, but her petulance could only have been assumed as an excuse for further ridicule, for she went on with mischievous enjoyment:

"How does he tick, Laura? Does he make love as well as Perry?"

"I wouldn't know," said Laura coolly, and Cleo aimed a petulant kick at her under the bedclothes.

"You can be quite infuriating when you like," she said crossly. "Have you fallen for Dom? He's just the type to raise flutters in virginal breasts."

Unicorns . . . young virgins as bait . . . thought Laura, and immediately blushed.

"O-oh!" exclaimed Cleo delightedly. "So that went home, did it? Well, don't set your sights too high darling. I may have use for Big Brother myself. Those conditions you mentioned. Didn't it really occur to you that he might have had me in mind? It would, after all, be quite a tidy solution of both our needs, wouldn't it? A wife for him and a father for Nicky. I rather think it's been mentioned before."

Laura remembered those other not very serious conversations with Cleo throwing out idle hints, but she remembered, too, that she had said there were more ways than one of killing a cat, and that if she was clever she could both have her cake and eat it is well.

"Would you bear his children?" she asked, with such unexpected sternness that Cleo blinked.

"Really, darling! Your imagination does leap ahead!" she replied, sounding slightly nonplussed. "But if you must have an answer to such a delicate question, it's no."

"That's cheating. What would he be getting in exchange for Troy's child?" Laura said, and temper showed in Cleo's eyes.

"You're hardly being very complimentary, sweetie-pie. Don't you consider *I* qualify as fair exchange, or is this sudden excess of primness simply a matter of sour grapes?" she snapped with some acidity.

Laura was silent, retreating into that semblance of abstraction which had long been a useful defence against unwelcome probing, but she probed for herself, nonetheless, and found the truth distasteful.

"Cleo, you and Perry—" she began, but Cleo, having scored the final hit in this rather unsatisfactory exchange, was bored with the subject.

"Oh, forget it," she said. "We've both been talking hot air. Did you know Perry's always had an urge for Australia? Troy over again. It's a grand country for adventurous spirits—better than this tax-ridden dump. I wouldn't mind going back there."

"Well, there's nothing to stop you, is there?" said Laura, suddenly feeling tired and rather cross, and Cleo's smile was provocative.

"Only the small matter of Nicky's future. Once that's settled, who knows? But then, of course, these mysterious conditions the head of the family is apparently preparing to lay down may necessitate my remaining here, mayn't they? Oh, stop looking like a bewildered sheep, Laura, and go and get Nicky up. Dom's promised to take him over the works after lunch. God knows why, so for heaven's sake try to get the brat into a reasonable frame of mind."

But Nicky was in a good mood, Laura found, when she went to the nursery to dress him. With cunning reminders of the night his Uncle Dom had told him a story, and hints that if he was as good as gold during the treat proposed for him, there might be another story forthcoming on the way home, she persuaded him into a most obliging state of mind.

The visit to the quarry turned out a failure, however, thanks to Cleo's last-minute decision to go with them.

They returned to the house a couple of hours later, inevitably disenchanted, and it was hard to say which was the crossest, the small boy or his mother.

Laura put a tearful small boy to bed after obliging with the promised story which his Uncle Dom had never told him in the end, then she slipped out of the house to enjoy the rest of the afternoon in blissful solitude.

She had presumed Dominic had gone back to the quarry after dropping his passengers at the house, but to her surprise his car still stood on the drive, and he himself appeared suddenly from the stable yard, the bunch of dogs at his heels.

"Hullo," she said, "I thought you'd gone back to the works."

"No," he replied, "I wanted a breath of air. Were you going for a walk? Well, we might as well join forces."

He did not sound enthusiastic, and Laura suspected that, like herself, he had planned to walk alone. It was awkward that having met inadvertently at precisely the same moment, they could do no less than go together as far as the gates. Once on the headland, however, she hung back to see which direction he would take and said firmly:

"I'm going this way. See you later."

To her surprise he turned in his tracks, whistling up the dogs, and fell into step beside her.

"Was that a brush-off?" he asked with a hint of the old arrogance, just as Peregrine might have, and she glanced up at him with faint apprehension.

"No," she said, "I had the idea you wanted to be alone."

"Meaning you did, I suppose. Well, Miss Mouse, you'll just have to put up with my company, I'm afraid."

They walked in silence after that, and he, as usual,

strode ahead without troubling to moderate his pace.

"I'm sorry the quarry visit didn't work out," she said, giving him a chance to work off his grievance. "Didn't Nicky behave?"

"Nicky? Oh, the boy was all right. He got a bit peeved when his mother wouldn't let him get as dirty as he liked, but that was only natural. I'd promised he should dig like a proper quarryman, and he felt cheated."

"You must take him again."

"No, I don't think so. Too many of the men remember that ancient quarrel. The older ones shared my father's view, you see. They think it's weakness to let bygones be bygones."

"Oh! You mean they resent Troy's wife and child?"

"In a sense. To them Cleo's a foreigner. The story wasn't a pretty one, and Cornishmen have long memories."

"No, it wasn't pretty. You—you must have cared very much, Dominic, to—to offer to take your brother's place—or am I trespassing again?"

"Trespassing? No, I don't think you'd ever do that, Laura," he said, shortening his stride as if he had only just become aware of her beside him, and as he looked down at her and she met the grave regard of those very blue eyes, she knew he was released from his bitterness. "Yes, I cared, but I was younger then."

"Only seven years."

"Well, seven years can be a long time. One changes."

"Yes, I suppose so. Like little Bridget," Laura said with a return to her natural habit of expecting people to follow her private train of thought, and Dominic raised an enquiring eyebrow.

"Who's she?" he asked. "One of your unlucky school friends crossed in love?"

"No one real—just something I once learnt.

> 'They stole little Bridget
> For seven years long;
> When she came down again,
> Her friends were all gone . . .' "

95

"Dear me! What an unfortunate happening for the poor girl! What happened to her after that?"

> " 'They took her lightly back,
> Between the night and morrow,
> They thought that she was fast asleep
> But she was dead with sorrow . . .' "

"Yes," he said, "that can happen too." The banter had gone from his voice and his smile was a little twisted. Laura looked up at him with eyes that were big with compassion. They had both come to a standstill and she was unaware of how much her transparent face revealed of her thoughts until he put a hand under her chin.

"No, Laura, you absurd, romantic creature, I haven't buried what passes for my heart in someone else's grave. You were implying that the other day in the stableyard when I bit you, weren't you? In any case, the lady is very much alive and happily wed to another, so I understand," he said, and she smiled again.

"Oh! What a good thing," she said with that cheerful matter-of-fact little air that he found rather touching. "And I'm not at all romantic in that sense, Dominic, even if I do seem absurd to you."

"Have you never been in love?" He asked the question with faint amusement, winding a strand of her hair absently round his finger, but she answered quite seriously:

"No, but then I don't meet many young men. Cleo's always been the honey that attracts the flies."

It was a pity, she thought, as she saw his change of expression, that she had mentioned Cleo. His earlier mood seemed to return, and he made no attempt to pursue the conversation. Whistling up the dogs, he turned for home, and they walked back in silence.

Supper was late that evening. Dominic had gone back to the works for a couple of hours to wind up some unfinished business which the earlier visit had interrupted, but he was kept longer than had been anticipated and by the time he and Peregrine returned, Cleo was in a contrary mood.

"Why the hell are the men so late?" she said impatiently, glancing at the clock, and Laura wondered if a prearranged date with Peregrine was in danger of being wrecked by the lateness of the hour, for Cleo had dressed with more than due care for the average evening at home and was becoming increasingly restless.

"I don't like Dom's foreman, he has an insolent way of looking at you," she said suddenly.

"That's just the natural Cornish suspicion of foreigners, I expect," Laura replied, but it would have been best left unsaid. An angry flush mounted under Cleo's warm, olive skin, and she said sharply:

"Has Dom been talking to you? Yes, of course—you dragged him out for a walk, didn't you?"

"As a matter of fact, I didn't. I would have much preferred to go alone, but we happened to meet."

"And he, I suppose, told you all about the scene with Perry over that business of Nicky."

"No, he didn't mention it. Was there a scene?"

"There's always a scene when Perry shows off, and the men just stood around and smirked. I could have choked Nicky for being so craven."

"I thought you said that Perry did it on purpose. Dom wouldn't have made the same mistake, you said."

"Oh, for heaven's sake, Laura, don't go throwing things back at me. I had a lecture on child psychology most of the way home, though he succumbed sufficiently to my humble plea for guidance to suggest a dinner in the town, and now it's too late."

So it was Dominic for whom Cleo had dressed with such care, thought Laura, and knew an irrational sense of disgust.

Peregrine breezed into the room, and his brother followed more leisurely, discarding his jacket and slinging it over a chair with the comfortable habit of years. He looked tired, Laura thought, but the earlier tension had gone out of him and he accepted Cleo's offer to mix him a drink with a small amused lift of eyebrows.

"What a change to become a guest in one's own house," he said, slipping down the knot of his tie and loosening his collar with, thought Laura, a rather pointed reminder that he was, nevertheless, master in his own home, but Cleo, who was not sensitive to nuances, smiled on him with the gracious indulgence of the lady of the house and asked what had kept them.

"How well you do it, dear sister-in-law," mocked Peregrine, and she smiled up at him with his own unruffled impudence.

"Our ties by marriage give me rights, don't you think?" she said, and slewed her bright eyes round to Dominic with the natural assurance of a woman whose charming liberties were never questioned. "Do you think I usurp your privileges, Dom? Do I make myself too much at home?"

"If you can put up with our somewhat uncouth manners in what technically should be the drawing-room, we, I'm sure, can bear with a little female possessiveness," Dominic said with a faint twinkle, and Cleo pouted.

"Was that a crack?" she said. "I'm quite equal to the brash harshness of the Trevaynes, which is more than my nicely brought up little cousin is."

"Not the best way to catch a unicorn, I fear," murmured Peregrine, with a rather unholy grin, and winked as he met Laura's surprised stare.

If Cleo heard, the remark did not register, and she looked at Dominic with a little pout.

"Had you forgotten we were going out?" she asked, and he smiled at her kindly.

"No, I hadn't forgotten, but it's too late now. There aren't many places round here where you can get a decent meal, anyway. Does our humdrum life bore you, Cleo?"

"I'd hardly call it humdrum with Trevayne passions ready to relieve the monotony by waxing high, but that I enjoy. As you've told me more than once, Dom, I measure up to family standards."

"Do you? Yes, perhaps you do. In fact—"

"In fact?" prompted Cleo, her eyes dancing.

"In fact this whole conversation's becoming a bore. If you and Cleo want a monopoly it's a pity you don't take her down to the local and have a cosy get-together," interrupted Peregrine rudely, and Laura looked at him curiously. He was jealous, she thought, really jealous under that familiar manner he adopted with his brother, and Dominic knew it, too, for he refrained from comment and merely grinned back with tolerant amusement.

The meal was tepid owing to the delay, but only Cleo picked discontentedly at her food. The other three, although they lapsed into their usual silence while occupied with eating, seemed on the other hand to relax, and Laura stared at the lamp in sleepy contemplation and remembered an old thatched farmhouse where once when she was a little girl, she and Auntie Flo had spent a summer's holiday.

"Who stole her?" asked Dominic suddenly, looking across the table at Laura.

"Who stole who?" she answered, puzzled.

"Little Bridget."

"Oh, her—the fairies, of course."

"Of course! I might have known."

"For heaven's sake!" exclaimed Cleo. "What next!"

"Yes, what next?" asked Dominic quite seriously. "Why was she stolen?"

"I don't quite know. It was the little men, according to the poem. They had frogs for their watchdogs," Laura answered with equal seriousness, and Bella suddenly spoke in bell-like tones:

" 'Up the airy mountain, down the rushy glen' . . . I remember . . . 'we daren't go a'hunting for fear of little men . . .' There were little men here in the mines, dear child—mischievous creatures called the knackers. They had to be appeased with offerings of food and light by the tinners, who were intensely superstitious. I wonder would there be any connection?"

Dominic said reflectively:

"Oh yes, there was such a race of little men, I believe, though they were more likely offshoots of the tinners themselves, who, in those days, lived such subhuman lives underground. Can you remember any more of your jingle, Laura?"

By now Laura had her elbows on the table and her chin propped on her hands. It must be the lamplight, she supposed, that was fostering such uncharacteristic topics.

"Not really," she said, trying to remember. "It was a very long poem. Something about an old king on a hilltop . . .'"

> "'High on the hill-top
> The old King sits;
> He is now so old and grey,
> He's nigh lost his wits!'"

Bella quoted triumphantly, and Cleo pushed back her chair with a grating scrape of impatience.

"I shall lose mine if you all indulge in much more whimsy," she said tartly. "Really, Dom! I wouldn't have expected you to support Laura's tiresome love of nonsense."

Too late Laura realised that, in Cleo's present mood, it had been the height of tactlessness to draw attention to herself.

"Wouldn't you, Cleo?" Dominic replied, sounding abstracted, and she gave a hard little laugh.

"No, I wouldn't. The Trevaynes, on their own showing, are of the earth, earthy—or are you, perhaps, just amusing yourself unkindly at my gullible cousin's expense?"

"You're in danger of over-playing your hand," he said very quietly, and Cleo suddenly hit out at him. He caught her wrists firmly in one hand, and as they stared into each other's eyes for a long, silent moment, Laura gave a little shiver. They were, she realised, oblivious for the moment, of the fact that they were not alone, and that mutual spark of passion, and Dominic's savage "Behave yourself! I'm not Perry!" seemed to reveal a closer acquaintanceship with one another than the casual exchanges of everyday life would have led one to suspect, or perhaps it was merely a hangover from the unsatisfactory afternoon.

Cleo laughed again with pleasurable unconcern, as Dominic let her go, and glancing across at Peregrine's derisive face, Laura saw he was unsurprised. Derision mingled with bitter amusement and he sat back lazily, as if watching a play, idly flipping bread pellets across the table.

The old hound came shuffling round Cleo's chair for attention, and she dropped him a chicken bone, only to have Dominic round on her with irritable displeasure.

"Don't you know better than to give a dog chicken-bones? They splinter and can pierce the intestines," he snapped, and Cleo jumped up, stretching her body with an impatient twist as though there was still a surplus store of energy to be released.

"Let's go out," she said to Peregrine. "Let's find the bright lights for an hour or two—since Dom won't take me."

"The pubs will be shut," said Dominic. "We were late with supper."

"Then let's take the car and drive around. You'll let me drive, won't you, Perry? She's a honey, that bus of yours—Troy would have loved her."

Laura wondered if Troy had been a deliberate reminder of her kinship with them, and for a moment she thought Peregrine was going to refuse rudely, then he got to his feet with a suddenness that sent his chair crashing to the floor and swaggered from the room, pulling Cleo after him.

Laura remained sitting, her hands folded under the table like an apprehensive little girl awaiting adult permission to get down. Dominic's eyes remained fixed on the closed door for a minute, a frown drawing his eyebrows into a straight, uncompromising black line, then he seemed to become aware of Laura sitting there so mutely and the frown deepened.

"Well, it's been quite a day, one way and another, hasn't it?" he said, getting up from the table. "Bella, you'd better see that Amos hasn't forgotten to put lamps in the girls' rooms before we go to bed."

"When I was a girl we had to make do with candles," Bella replied with her oblique method of answering a question. "Winding-sheets . . . I can remember them still . . . such a satisfactory reminder of the decay of the flesh."

"Winding-sheets?" Laura echoed, her eyes growing

big at this final touch of the macabre, and Dominic on his way to the door, said without turning his head:

"The melted wax that runs down the sides, Miss Mouse of the literal mind. Even Bella wasn't compelled to go to bed in her shroud. Goodnight."

CHAPTER SEVEN

BY morning the incident should have appeared no more to Laura than the trifling flare-ups Penzion had accustomed her to, but she was not, she realised, able to stand outside Trevayne affairs so easily as when she had first come. Her relations with Dominic had shifted almost imperceptibly to another plane, as, she thought, had his with her. She did not want to become personally involved with this strange household so alien to her known background, but their varying small demands on her would no longer permit her to stand apart, and her own awakening fondness for Dominic was a factor that disturbed her.

"How does one know?" she asked Bella, the day after that uncomfortable sequence of events resulting from Nicky's visit to the works.

The day was Good Friday, for Easter was late that year. The Zion Works would be traditionally closed for a week, and Laura had looked forward with slight trepidation to day upon day of unrelieved Trevayne company.

"Know what, dear child?" said Bella with obliging attention, but clearly more interested in continuing with the linen they were sorting together in the little annexe off the kitchen which had once been the still-room.

"I don't quite know," Laura said, and indeed she had no idea why her vagrant thoughts should have led her to near self-betrayal.

"Of course you don't," Bella answered with a soothing rejection of confidences not yet ripe for dissection. "When one is young, so many imagined problems . . . so many perplexities . . . but it all sorts out, you know."

"Does it?"

"When one is young," Bella continued, inspecting a pile of clearly forgotten assortments of unmatching table mats with some surprise, "everything seems complex, but so little really is, except the ordinary demands of life like the lights failing and fleas in the dogs and the elastic in one's knickers giving out at the most *awkward* moment—don't you agree?"

Peregrine, putting his head round the door in time to hear Bella's last observation, asked with interest whose knickers were giving out.

"If it's yours, Miss Bread-and-butter, I'll stand by to watch the fun," he said, grimacing at Laura. It was perhaps unfortunate that Dominic also happened to be passing and was clearly in no mood for banter.

"Can't you keep your prep school humour for more appropriate occasions?" he said as he went on his way, and Peregrine made a rude noise.

"What's eating Big Brother of late?" he demanded of Bella. "Can it be that our innocent Laura has managed to get under his skin, despite the more obvious attractions of cousin Cleo? I always told him, you know, that he was the protective type."

"Did you, dear boy?" said Bella without surprise. "Well, that's scarcely your own discovery. Dom is the only one of the three of you with a touch of his mother's tenderness."

"Well, for crying out loud!" Peregrine exclaimed, slapping her on her ample posterior. "Are you going over to the enemy at this late stage?"

"Do you think of Dominic as the enemy, then?" Bella asked, fixing him for a moment with that pale, china-blue gaze and he gave a little shrug.

"Not really, I suppose. He just needles me," he said, like a small boy shamed for once into honesty, then catching Laura's wide-eyed look of troubled uncertainty, he tweaked her hair and added with the old banter: "Laura, I have a notion, shares your partisanship, Bella, old girl. Is it possible, do you think, she cherishes a secret weakness for the predatory overlord? Look! She's blushing!"

Laura, aware of that treacherous colour, was too much occupied with a renewal of disquieting suspicions regarding her own emotions to make her customary retort, but Bella remarked with dispassionate calm:

"That may or may not be, dear boy, but nothing, surely, to cause amazement. A weakness is one thing—a *tendresse* quite another."

"Right as always, you wise old faggot," he acknowledged handsomely, and winked at Laura, but joining Cleo a little later on the terrace where it was warm enough now to sit out in the midday sun, he observed, with the provocative lack of preamble that could always throw her off guard, that it wouldn't at all surprise him if Brother Dom wasn't at last in danger of being hooked.

Cleo, rather prematurely wooing a becoming tan, preened herself complacently and retorted:

"Why not? Don't you think I'd be good enough for the head of the house? We would make a rather striking couple, don't you think?"

Peregrine sat down on one of the stone benches that rather incongruously dotted these flowerless gardens, and his expression was not pleasant.

"I was referring to the little cousin, not to you," he said, taking pleasure in the angry colour creeping under her skin. "That little exhibition of yours last night at supper might strike sparks off Troy and me, but it isn't the bait to catch Dom with, despite his blood, as I think I told you later."

"It struck sparks all right!"

"But not the right ones."

"You were jealous," she snapped, and his smile broadened.

"Oh, I was jealous all right—you intended that, didn't you? Are you seriously making a play for the head boy?"

"Why not? I want security for myself as well as for my son. I'm tired of being unattached."

"How virtuous you sound when you allude to your son instead of to the brat. You don't care a damn for him, do you?"

"I try, but I must confess children bore me. They bored Troy, too—they would bore you, Perry, and that's probably why—"

"I won't marry you? I admire your honesty, I must own, but your importunate brat isn't the only stumbling block."

"What then?"

"You know very well. I don't want to be tied."

"Aren't you tied to Dom and the quarry and the

whole tiresome family set-up so long as you remain?"

"There's that, of course. Still and all—"

"Still and all, I don't mind betting if Nicky was out of the way, you'd sing a different tune," Cleo said, and rolled on to her back, spread-eagling her limbs with sensuous pleasure on the rug laid out on the grass.

"Perhaps," he said. It would, he knew, take more than his too-familiar taunts and pinpricks to shake that colossal self-confidence, so he returned to the original bait.

"You don't seem to take the prospect of a rival very seriously," he said with gentle venom, and smiled at the instinctive little kick of annoyance she gave with one foot.

"Hardly, if it's Laura you're referring to," she snapped.

"Who else? You'd scarcely consider Bella a serious stumbling block at her age, would you?"

"Don't be fatuous! I'll admit it's crossed my mind that poor Laura might be succumbing to a weakness for an imagined hero of her adolescent day-dreams, but she'll get over it."

He laughed a little cruelly.

"Bella has just informed me that a weakness is one thing and a *tendresse* is quite another. She seems to think Dom is capable of both—one leading to the other, so to speak. Quite a thought, isn't it?"

"Really, Perry! You know quite well what Bella is when she's got some bee in her bonnet!"

"This one might be buzzing to some purpose, my pretty, if you care to look for the signs. Can't you tell them, or don't you want to? Haven't you noticed the observant eye in the background guarding the ewe lamb from contamination with our sleazy pubs, and being mindful of youth and innocence, etc., etc.?"

"That's no reason for assuming anything deeper. He treats her like a child and is probably merely very conscious of that tiresome sense of responsibility he has come to take so seriously. In any case, Laura's much too dumb to make the running, even if she had any inkling of success."

"Oh, I grant you that. The poor sweet's scarcely dry

106

behind the ears yet, as Dom once pointed out when telling me to lay off."

"Well, there you are, then. All this childish nonsense to draw red herrings," said Cleo comfortably, and he looked down at her with the cynical eyes of a man who, despite recognition of his own worthlessness, admits a reluctance to break entirely free.

"So you'd marry Dom, if you could get him, in spite of what's been between us?" he asked, with curiosity rather than regret, and she smiled at him lazily.

"What makes you think I won't get him?" she said. "I hold the trump card. He wants Nicky."

"What in hell do you mean?"

"He told Laura he would like to bring the boy up here—on certain conditions. It might be reasonably supposed, don't you think, that the conditions could include me? After all, if one's to believe gossip, the love of the poor man's life was the girl Troy took from him, so conventional reasons for marriage are quite in order. He needs heirs, and if I don't inspire undying love I can certainly stir the more primitive passions, as you'll agree."

"Oh, yes, my charming trollop, I'll agree, but I hardly think you'd oblige so readily in the matter of heirs."

"Of course not, but who's to say where that fault would lie? Nicky would make up. And why should you care, Perry? You'll still be living here. You'll be in the enviable position of having your cake and eating it, just as I intend to do."

For a moment his eyes lost their habitual boldness and were the eyes of a man shocked into unfamiliar disgust.

"You really *are* a tramp, aren't you?" he said quite quietly, and she gave him a quick, uncertain look.

"I'm amoral, which is perhaps a little different," she retorted coolly. "Don't forget Troy taught me his own code of ethics, which is why we made a go of marriage, despite his roving temperament. I don't mind betting, either, that you wouldn't stand out for loyalty if it came to the test."

"Oh, no, I'll grant you that," he replied with the old impudence. "Between us, we'd make a good show of cheating the poor blighter all round, wouldn't we?"

She stretched with cat-like indolence, and smiled at him across the slowly tightening material across her full, firm breasts.

"Cheating?" she said, and wrinkled her nose at him.

"Certainly. Fun for me, and no heirs for him. Charming!"

"Laura threw that at me, too. I didn't know then, of course, she was cherishing a hopeless passion for Dom."

"Don't be so sure it's hopeless, my pretty Cleo. Look at that," Peregrine said with malicious amusement.

Dominic and Laura were coming round the side of the house, walking with the leisurely familiarity of old friends, or even of tomorrow's lovers. Dominic's earlier ill-humour seemed to have left him, for he had an arm round Laura's shoulders and she was laughing up at him. As they neared the terrace where Cleo and Peregrine were still hidden from them, he suddenly picked her up to lift her over a low wall and held her, for a moment, high in his arms.

"How light you are!" he said as he set her down again, and smoothed a disordered strand of her hair back into place with an unconscious little gesture of tenderness.

"What a touching display of gallantry. Laura *is* capable of stepping over low walls herself, you know," Cleo said with, she realised as she saw the amused expression on both men's faces, a too hasty petulance.

"*Miaow!*" squeaked Peregrine with such lifelike imitation of a cat that the dogs sprang up, barking hysterically. The smallest of the bitches, a fawning, subservient creature without much charm, caught a good-natured kick from Peregrine in passing and promptly flung herself on her back in an ecstasy of apology and worship.

"That's women for you—treat 'em rough and they always come back for more!" Peregrine said, "It's the secret of Trevayne success with the fair sex, isn't it, Dom?"

"Speak for yourself. I don't go in for that sort of courtship," Dominic said good-temperedly, but his eyes idly rested with rather an odd expression on Laura, who found herself thinking that, if sufficiently aroused to anger, the dark Trevayne would not be too particular what methods he employed to ram home his authority.

Bella came out to tell them lunch was nearly ready and if someone would shut the dogs up, Nicky could join them for five minutes before he sat down to his own.

"Oh, I'd forgotten him!" Laura exclaimed remorsefully. "Cleo, you should have reminded me to fetch him down."

"You're his temporary nanny, it's up to you to remember," Cleo retorted with good-humoured indifference. "But I'll confess, I forgot him myself, poor brat, and it really is time he got over his fear of the dogs."

"He's getting much better. It only needs a little more time and patience. He's afraid of being knocked over, which is understandable when you consider his size," Laura said.

"Is anyone going into Merrynport tomorrow?" Bella asked, as Dominic went off to the kennels, the pack at his heels.

"I'd thought of going to the races. Why? Forgotten to order in enough food for the holiday, you vague old faggot?" said Peregrine, and Bella looked even more vague.

"No, there should be enough with the capons and lamb, and I shall make a giant pasty with plenty of potatoes and onions. I was thinking of eggs."

"Eggs! For God's sake! We've got enough hens of our own, haven't we?"

"Yes, dear boy, of course. I mean *Easter* eggs. I know we never bother with such things, but we have a child in the house now."

"Don't bother on Nicky's account—we've never kept Easter, either," said Cleo, and Laura said, grateful for Bella's support:

"But that's sad, Cleo. Chocolate eggs and fluffy chickens were such fun when one was small. Is there a bus to Merrynport on a Saturday, Bella?"

"I'll drive you in. We'll make a do of it and rope in Dom and have lunch there. I can go racing on

109

Monday," Peregrine said, but Cleo, doubtless reminded of Dominic's cancelled invitation of the night before, turned sulky.

"Take Laura if you want to, but count me out. Dom and I can put our feet up here and spend a more rewarding afternoon than poking about for crummy Easter eggs," she said, and Peregrine's smile was mocking.

"Right!" he said. "You do that little thing, my pretty, and try your hand at diplomacy—or would seduction be a better definition? Laura and I have never had a jaunt on our own, have we, Miss Bread-and-butter? I for one will look forward to the binge. Are you going to bring the brat out, Bella, or shall I go and fetch him?"

"I shall go and dye some eggs," Bella answered with disappointing matter-of-factness, and went into the house.

Laura set off with Peregrine the next morning as pleased as a child given an unexpected treat. The warm weather was an excuse to wear a pretty dress, and her doubts of yesterday were forgotten, or pushed aside, for the day was fine and warm, trips into Merrynporth were rare enough to provide mild excitement, and there was a holiday feeling in the air.

Cleo's day, however, did not turn out quite as she had planned, though later she flattered herself that she had not entirely wasted her opportunities. She waved the other two off with fond wishes for their mutual enjoyment, but Dominic stood watching the car shave the gates with Peregrine's usual careless flourish, a frown between his eyes.

"Whose idea was this?" he asked. "Perry was supposed to be giving me a hand with some fencing that came down in one of the gales."

"I don't know—maybe Laura's—she doesn't get out much. Let's have a drink. Dom," Cleo said, and didn't think it necessary to explain about the Easter shopping.

"It's too early for me, but I'll mix you one if you like," he replied without enthusiasm, and she slipped a hand through his arm, coaxing him back into the house.

"Don't be a spoilsport, Dom," she said. "Why shouldn't Laura have her bit of fun? I've been rather selfish, monopolising all the outings, besides—I'm afraid she's lost her heart a bit to Perry."

He frowned again.

"To Perry? I rather gathered the impression that his crude advances didn't cut much ice."

"Oh, that's just Laura's little way. Most girls put up a smoke-screen if their emotions are getting involved. Laura's impressionable and not very experienced, and Perry's damned attractive."

"Yes, I'd rather thought you found him so," he observed a little dryly, and she gave him a slow, knowledgeable smile as she arranged herself elegantly in a chair by one of the open windows of the tea-room.

"Me? But of course I do—all the Trevaynes are hellishly attractive—but I know my way around. I cut my first teeth on Troy, so Perry's no danger to me now, but Laura has yet to learn. Aren't you going to pour me that drink, darling?"

"Perry's not a very good subject on which to cut one's teeth," he said, walking over to the drink trolley.

"Why should you care? Laura's not your responsibility," she said, accepting the drink he had poured for her, and raising her glass to him in a small gesture of salute.

"Don't you consider she's yours?" he asked, balancing himself on the window-ledge and jingling the loose coins in his trouser pocket. "You seem to be the child's sole surviving relative."

The small, clinking noise irritated her. "I wish you'd have a drink, Dom. It's so cheerless imbibing alone. Laura? Well, yes, in a way I suppose I do feel responsible, for the poor sweet is a bit dumb in some ways, but there's been a long gap, you know, and she's entitled to live her own life, don't you think? Besides, darling, I'm in no position to make a home for her, if that's what you're thinking—I've no home myself."

"But you're a nomad, I suspect, Cleo," he said, and got up and went back to the trolley as if on second thoughts he had decided to relax. "You enjoyed your racketing life in Australia, didn't you?"

She shot him a quick look, wondering what the right answer was to that, but his back was turned to her while he measured himself a whisky and she said reflectively:

"Oh yes, it's a great country for the young. But money was tight, and a child can be a handicap if you have to live rough."

"Did you ever live rough?" he countered with a hint of scepticism, and she looked surprised.

"Oh yes, if I had to. Don't you believe I can measure up to your roughneck pattern?" she said, and he smiled as he settled himself opposite her with his drink.

"Yes, on second thoughts, I think you can, and probably outdo the lot of us," he said. "Would you go back?"

"To Australia?" She lowered her lashes and observed him through them. He was, perhaps, only talking idly to fill in a too-long period before lunch, but Dominic, she knew, seldom asked questions that required no answers.

"Perhaps, had things been different," she said. "But Troy's dead, Nicky needs security and—I think I do, too."

He considered her reflectively, those very blue eyes a rather uncomfortable reminder that there was a streak in him which did not conform to the pattern she knew. By mentioning the boy with such a frank invitation for discussion she had given him an opening to suggest those nebulous plans of which Laura had spoken, but he ignored the opening; or possibly the time was not ripe, and merely enquired when Laura was expected back.

"For heaven's sake, how should I know?" she snapped back exasperated. "Really, Dom, you're behaving like a maiden aunt who expects the worst from an unchaperoned outing! Laura may be a bit dumb, but she's not halfwitted, even if she does fancy herself in love."

"Isn't it you who's making rather a to-do?" he said coolly. "I merely asked when they were expected back.

I was thinking of that fencing I want to get repaired, you see. Have another drink."

She gave him her glass, annoyed with her own self-betrayal and with his stubborn refusal to react.

"I can quite understand why Laura finds you difficult," she said waspishly.

"Does she?"

"Of course. You make her nervous."

"I know I do. It's an unfortunate effect I have on strangers, I'm afraid."

"But not on me, darling," she said, sure of her ground again, as he gave her back her replenished glass. "I can stand up to any of you."

"Oddly enough, so can your cousin," he replied with a reminiscent twinkle, and Cleo got the impression that she had mysteriously lost ground.

"Oh, Laura was always one for answering back, even if she was scared stiff," she said. "If she's more reserved with you, it's only natural, isn't it? Perry's so much nearer her own age and he has the advantage of being pin-up boy at the moment."

She had the satisfaction of seeing that shaft go home. She should have remembered earlier that a man coming rather late in life to the imagined attractions of youth was always sensitive about his age.

Laura and Peregrine got back just as it was growing dusk. Peregrine was making such a racket on the horn that Cleo went out on to the porch, meeting Dominic in his shirt-sleeves returning from his solitary wrestling with the broken fencing, and they stood together, watching the car turn into the drive with the familiar squeal of tyres. Laura was perched in the back on the folded hood, her hair streaming in the wind, her skirt above her knees; Peregrine wore a funny hat. Both were singing, and Laura gave a shriek as the car came to a violent halt and only just saved herself from falling off backwards.

"For heaven's sake!" exclaimed Cleo. "Has Perry got the poor girl tiddly?"

Dominic waited in an ominous silence for his brother to get out, but Peregrine began collecting a vast number of parcels together and shouted cheerfully to Dominic to come and help.

Laura continued to sit on the hood, loth, it would seem, to abandon her commanding perch. Her arms were clasped round her knees now, and she smiled beatifically down upon the men and let them do the work.

"No stops on the way home?" Dominic asked with a thoughtful eye on Laura.

"Nary a one, but your ewe lamb's drunk all right—drunk with sheer delight. It's an amazing phenomenon."

"Did you know, Dominic, the fun of those stalls on the waterfront? The winkles and the jellied eels and the funny hats and monkeys on sticks? Look, I've brought one for Nicky, but I think I shall keep it myself," Laura said, diving down to the back seat to retrieve the toy and show him how it worked. Her eyes were brilliant, and her hair in wild disorder, and she had kicked her shoes off into the bottom of the car. She was indeed drunk, thought Dominic, drunk with a bubbling inner happiness that was quite new to him, and he experienced an odd little prick of anger when Peregrine picked her up and swung her over the side with a good-natured injunction to wake up, and she stood for a moment to let her hands linger on his shoulders.

"Thank you, Perry," she said softly. "Thank you for a wonderful day."

Some of the day's magic still remained with Laura as she sat down with the others for the evening meal, and she scarcely noticed that the eager recounting of all they had done was rather coolly received by Dominic. He shut himself up in the book-room as soon as the meal was finished, and Laura, aware that Cleo at any rate was finding the presence of a third person distinctly irksome, took herself off to an early bed.

Because Dominic had made her free of the book-room, she paused there to say goodnight and to tell him she had bought Easter presents on his behalf to give to Nicky the next day.

"Because," she said, standing in the doorway, not as yet sure of her welcome, "I didn't think you'd remember, as it must be a long time since you looked forward to chocolate eggs and hares and chickens and things."

"You don't need to remind me that I'm too old to remember my childhood," he replied with such unexpected sharpness that she looked bewildered.

"I'm sorry," she said, uncertain whether to retire hastily or try to explain. "I—I wasn't suggesting you were too old; I only thought you might have forgotten, not being used to children."

"Quite right," he said, getting to his feet. "If I'd known the main object of the expedition, I'd have come with you. Come in, Laura, if you want to."

The invitation sounded formal rather than cordial, but she came in, leaving the door open as an idication that she did not mean to stay.

"Didn't Cleo tell you?" she said. "Perry originally suggested we all should go and make a sort of party of it, but she didn't want to. Shall I tell you what I've bought for you, Dominic?"

"If you like. But why not lump all the offerings together, and let the boy sort them out for himself? He'll hardly care who's given him what."

"Oh! Well, if you'd rather . . . I just thought it would be nice if you gave him your presents personally. I chose specially nice ones for you."

"Bribery? I hardly think a few eggs and a couple of plastic chickens or so will win me to the good graces of my nephew," he said with such cool irony that she flushed.

"They aren't plastic! The chicken is soft and fluffy and has lovely velvet feet and the other's a baby rabbit with *real* fur—and I think you're hateful!" she said, and his face suddenly softened to the familiar amused tenderness that she had come to associate with him.

"Now I've hurt your feelings—or is it your commercial instinct that's outraged, my literal-minded Laura?" he said. "I didn't mean to sound ungrateful—or to spoil your day."

But he *had* spoilt it. She was aware now that something had upset him since the morning, and remembering that he and Cleo had been alone together for the best part of the day, she thought she knew what it was.

He had most likely broached whatever plans he had in mind for Nicky, and Cleo, being Cleo, would almost certainly have kept him guessing, just to make sure of him.

"You haven't spoilt my day," she assured him politely, but there was such a flat note of discouragement in her voice that he looked up quickly.

"Yes, I have. I've been rather childish and dog-in-the-manger, for reasons you wouldn't understand," he said, "Come here."

"I understand," she said, not moving.

"Do you? I wonder."

"Goodnight, Dominic," she said, and slipped out of the room like a little ghost.

Sunday was disappointingly wet, which kept them all in the house too long for tempers not to become frayed by the end of the day, and Laura's schemes for Nicky's amusement misfired with depressing flatness. She supposed she should have foreseen that Peregrine, with such material at hand to play the benevolent uncle lavishing presents and exciting surprises and playing tireless games, wouldn't miss an opportunity for putting his less inventive brother in the shade, but it hurt her to see Dominic's presents discarded in favour of others and his efforts to join in the fun rejected. By lunch time the boy was over-excited and cross, and everyone was thankful when he was put to bed in the nursery for his afternoon rest, but it was Peregrine, of course, who obliged with a piggyback up the stairs in answer to the demand to play unicorns.

"Why don't you go up for a bit and tell him a story like you did that night?" Laura suggested to Dominic, but was rewarded with a distinctly chilly look.

"You're mistaken if you think I'm prepared to bribe my way into a child's affections—or anyone else's for the matter of that. The boy's had too much attention as it is," he said, and took himself off, despite the rain, for a long tramp with the dogs.

Cleo and Peregrine were ensconced on a sofa in the tea-room with a very definite air of intimacy, and Laura, feeling unwanted by any of them, went out to the kitchen to help Bella wash up.

"It hasn't been a success, has it?" she said ruefully, drying while Bella washed. "We overdid it, of course, but I do wish Perry would sometimes take a back seat. I don't think he cares a hoot about Nicky, and Dominic does."

"It's only history repeating itself, dear child," said Bella dispassionately. "With this family it's always been the ones who didn't care who won the prizes. Perhaps you will break the chain."

"Me? I don't make an impression on any of them. How could I break the chain? I don't think I really understand what you're talking about, Bella."

"Very probably not. Still, dear child, remember the unicorn, won't you?"

"The unicorn?" For a moment Laura thought this must be one of Bella's more random remarks. She had not thought about the legend for some time, but now, remembering, she felt herself grow pink.

"You make things sound very mysterious," she said, and Bella absently started re-washing a plate that had already been dried.

"The best things in life *are* mysterious," she said. "Death is mysterious—and love—and birth. Do you care for Perry?"

Her quite ordinary queries were so often a tailpiece to more cryptic utterances that they invariably took you by surprise, Laura thought, not knowing quite what answer to make.

"I care for his company when he isn't showing off," she replied, "but I would find the Trevaynes too violent and unpredictable to live up to for very long."

They finished their chores in silence, Bella because abstraction had become a habit when there was nothing more to be said; Laura because her spirits seemed suddenly to drop to zero. Bella, she supposed, had been scattering hints in her odd, roundabout fashion, and Laura knew now that Dominic must have mentioned their discussion on Nicky's future and most likely been rather more explicit as to his intentions.

Her thoughts went to Peregrine and Cleo, most

probably at that moment making lazy love in the tea-room to while away a wet afternoon. Only that morning, going very early to the nursery with her Easter parcels, she had met Peregrine coming out of her cousin's room in dressing-gown and pyjamas. He had, of course, been quite unabashed and volunteered the information that he had taken Cleo an early cup of tea, but Laura knew that all the trays were still unused and waiting for Bella to make the tea at eight o'clock. She had no right or, indeed, any wish to censure her cousin's private life, but she found Cleo's willingness to accept marriage from one man while she took what she wanted from another difficult to stomach.

"I must be a prig I suppose," she said aloud, forgetting she was not alone as she spread out the teacloths to dry, and jumped when Bella answered:

"Not a prig, dear child—so smug and prim and without humour, don't you agree? And a prig is one thing and a virgin quite another." She made the pronouncement in exactly the same manner in which she had rebuked Peregrine for levity on the morning of Good Friday, and Laura hugged her, suddenly near to tears.

"Oh, dear Bella, you are so absurd, and I *do* love you," she said, and bolted from the kitchen to cry in private.

Dominic returned long after they had all finished tea and going upstairs to change out of his wet clothes met Laura coming down.

"We mustn't pass on the stairs, it's unlucky," she said with that solemn air she had when voicing superstitions, and he stretched out both hands to the banisters, barring her way.

"Then one of us will have to go back, won't we?" he said, "Which shall it be?"

"It's usual," she said, still in that serious voice, "for a man to give way to a lady."

"But I'm nearly at the top, and I'm soaking wet. You wouldn't like me to catch a chill, I'm sure," he said equally gravely, and she looked down on the black wet head, saw unsuspected grey threads in the disordered hair which was beginning to curl, and the smile in his very blue eyes, and felt her bones turn suddenly to water.

"You have some white hairs, did you know?" she said rather absurdly, unable to resist touching his hair with a quick involuntary movement.

"Oh, yes, I know. My shaving mirror points the horrid truth each morning," he replied with mock dismay, but although his voice was teasing, his face changed as he observed the traces of tears on hers, and he said quickly: "Has something upset you, Laura?"

"No—no, of course not," she answered, wondering if he would ever guess how he himself could upset her.

"Is it Perry?" he asked, and because in a sense it was Perry combined with Cleo who had caused her distress, she answered: "Perhaps," and saw his face harden.

"Perry's a charmer, but he's also a philanderer and and—unreliable. Remember that, Laura," he said curtly, and saw her eyes widen in surprise. Did he think it necessary to warn her of the obvious at this late stage? she wondered, but she said nothing, and almost at once he dropped his hands from the banisters and stood aside.

"I think we'll risk passing on the stairs, This house is accustomed to the flouting of superstitions and possibly bad luck," he said with an unexpected touch of bitterness, and she slipped past him and ran down the stairs.

The weather had cleared by nightfall and the next day was fine and dry as the most pessimistic Bank Holidaymaker could wish for.

"So nice for the workers," said Bella, who was in one of her rather county moods. "What are you going to do?"

"I shall take Nicky for his short walk along the headland," Laura said, and was surprised when Cleo said she would come too. She had never offered to accompany them before, and Laura, as they set out, hoped this was not an excuse for embarrassing confidences.

"You enjoyed your little spree with Perry, didn't you?" Cleo said as they made leisurely progress along the headland. "My day was productive, too. Things are progressing, darling."

"Yes?" said Laura, contemplating a circling gull overhead and wishing she was alone, but Cleo clearly had something she wished to unburden and it was better to encourage her and get it over with.

"Lay off Dom," she said suddenly and quite unexpectedly, and Laura turned to look at her.

"I don't know what you mean," she said, and Cleo laughed.

"Always the stock answer when one's caught out, isn't it?" she said, and Laura stopped to disentangle Nicky from a clinging brier.

"Look, Cleo," she said, "if you're trying to pick a quarrel over your future plans, leave me out. Dominic isn't interested in me in any way that can interfere with you, as you've frequently told me, and when you tell me to lay off you're rather suggesting something unpleasant."

Cleo kicked the turf with a petulant foot.

"Sorry, darling," she said, taking Laura's arm, "I didn't mean to suggest you were making a play for him, but you *have* got a bit of a crush, haven't you? And I wouldn't like your tender feelings to suffer, because if I mean to have him, you won't stand a chance."

The sky was an arc of purest blue above them and bees, the first sleepy promise of summer, were already beginning to plunder the blossoming gorse. A day, thought Laura gratefully, to remember when she had gone.

"Did he tell you his conditions for Nicky, then, on Saturday?" she asked rather flatly, and Cleo gave her arm a squeeze.

"Well, now, wouldn't you like to know?" she said. "I'll tell you this much, though. Dom and I quite clearly see eye to eye over Nicky's future, so that should answer you, shouldn't it?"

"No," said Laura, withdrawing her arm, and experiencing again the profound distaste of yesterday for the situation developing. "You're having an affair with Perry, aren't you?"

"Well, what of it? I tried to explain to you the other

day that once you're used to a husband, or a lover, it's hell to do without."

"Oh yes, I took the point, but—"

"But what? Are you trying to condemn something you can't possibly understand, never having been married?"

"No, of course not. I may seem to you, Cleo, tiresomely naïve and inexperienced, but I'm not ignorant. I know very well the importance of the physical side of marriage, and I can well imagine the needs and frustrations one might be faced with when that has gone, only—I just can't *take* this thing of yours to keep the best of both worlds. Do you really mean to go on as you are now if you do marry Dominic? Wouldn't you have any feeling of obligation to him—any loyalty to the—to the terms of your bargain?"

"Oh, belt up, darling, you talk like a tract!" said Cleo with an unamused laugh. "Don't, for heaven's sake, go dropping sly hints to Dom, hoping to queer my pitch. I've not made up my mind, anyway, what I'm going to do. I was simply warning you off the grass."

They walked on in silence, Cleo with a sulky face and an almost visible sense of grievance, Laura with a spirit temporarily soothed but not reassured. After a while, Cleo flung herself down on the grass, bored with their aimless walking, and Laura sat down on a convenient tussock beside her.

"Laura," Cleo said suddenly, stretching out a conciliatory hand, "bear with my bitchiness, darling. I'm so mixed up sometimes, and when I'm unsure, I snap."

"Mixed up—you?" exclaimed Laura with such surprise that Cleo gave an impatient shrug.

"Oh, come off it, Laura! It's no good either of us pretending that I'm still the glamourous, out-of-reach cousin who could do no wrong. You've grown up since those days, as I've told you before, and even if you're not very bright as yet where sex is concerned, you must at least know that we're all liable to get mixed up at times."

"Of course," Laura said gently, regretting with Cleo

that the old, unquestioning hero-worship had died with adolescence, and a little ashamed that she seemed unable to give the right assurance on the very rare occasions it was asked of her.

"Cleo," she began impulsively, trying to cling to this mutually adult moment between them, "it's Perry you really want, isn't it? He's Troy all over again for you, isn't he, and that must be hell. Dominic won't suffice, you know, even though he's worth ten of Perry."

That was a mistake, she saw at once, for Cleo flushed angrily.

"More good advice à la Auntie Flo? You're scarcely in a position to judge either of them as lovers, I imagine," she said waspishly. "We all know Perry gave you a bit of a whirl on Saturday, but I don't mind betting the careful Dom hasn't thrown his cap over the windmill—or has he?"

"Of course not—neither of them have," said Laura with distaste, and called an unnecessary warning to Nicky to stay away from the cliff's edge.

He had been playing quietly by himself near at hand, but having captured Laura's attention, he ran off into the scrub, inviting a game, and she rather thankfully jumped up and went after him. Presently, however, his shouts of delight turned to screams of fright as the Penzion dogs, returning from their walk with Peregrine, spied him and knocked him over, rolling him joyously in the bushes. Peregrine came striding after them through the gorse, and Laura, striving to extricate the child from a tangle of waving tails and affectionate tongues, half-laughingly shouting to him to call the dogs off.

"They wouldn't hurt him, they just want to play," Peregrine said, but he snapped a command to the dogs, who promptly lay down, panting at his feet. "See? Nicky ought to be used to the blighters by now. They wouldn't harm a fly. Nicky, come here."

Laura was on her knees, trying to soothe the terrified child, and Cleo joined her, looking down at her son with evident disgust, and making no move to intervene.

"Come here, Nicky," Peregrine said again, and held out his hands.

The boy hesitated, but his faith in the uncle who was always on his side was so complete that he stopped crying and made a tentative movement towards him.

"Come on—they won't hurt you," Peregrine coaxed him, and Nicky reached the reassuring hands. With one swift movement, his uncle snatched him up on high, and his wild yell of "Yoicks!" galvanised the quiescent dogs into a frenzy of leaping and barking. Nicky began to scream and struggle, and in all the noise Laura's frantic exhorations were hardly heard.

Peregrine, the boy on his shoulders, began walking towards the cliff's edge, the yelping dogs milling at his heels, and as he put one foot on a flat boulder on the very brink of an outjutting overhang in the rock, Laura knew a moment of irrational fear.

"What's he going to do? Stop him, Cleo!" she cried.

"Well, he's not going to hurl the unfortunate brat over the side, if that's what you're thinking," Cleo replied crushingly. "He's simply trying the well-known cure of shock treatment—throwing the child into the water to make it swim—remember?"

Laura closed her eyes, trying to control a futile impulse to make a dash for Peregrine and snatch the boy from him, and when she opened them again he was standing on the boulder, exhorting Nicky to be a man and laughingly threatening to drop him over the edge if he didn't stop bawling.

To Laura it seemed an age before Peregrine turned and stepped down off the boulder. As he did so, the dogs which had been poised with him, their heraldic outlines looking like a strange frieze against the sky, suddenly made off along the headland barking hysterically, and Laura turned to see Dominic's tall figure striding towards them.

"What the hell's going on here?" he shouted. "I could hear the boy's screams as far as the house; what's been going on?"

"Oh, it was just Nicky making an exhibition of himself because the dogs rolled him over," Cleo replied, lazy amusement in her husky voice. "Perry's cured him, I hope, by the good old-fashioned methods."

"It's not the right way—cruelty can never produce anything but fear," Laura said in a shocked, tight little voice, and Dominic, as he reached them, took a quick look at her white face which seemed swamped by those great eyes, unblinking and unnaturally wide.

"Sit down on the grass, Laura, I'll attend to you later," he ordered sharply, and she obeyed without further speech, reminded for no reason of that first meeting on the station platform when her legs had performed the same disconcerting trick of refusing to support her. Then he had picked her up and sat her on a bench, and later she had wept on his shoulder, though she couldn't remember why. She wanted to weep now, but the tears wouldn't come, which was a good thing, she thought, with a brief return to common sense. She was, of course, unacquainted with the initial stages of shock.

"And how, might I ask, do you suppose balancing on a rock on the edge of a cliff is going to cure a fear of animals?" Dominic was enquiring sarcastically, and at the dark fury in his voice even Cleo looked uneasy.

"That was the second lesson. You know he has this silly fear of heights, Dom," she said, and sounded quite surprised that such things had to be explained. He glanced at her for a second with a rather disturbing look and she added quickly: "Surely you agree that Nicky should grow up like the rest of you? He's such a typical Trevayne in looks, and I'm so desperately anxious that he should do you credit and grow to manhood in the old tradition."

"I think you really believe that, Cleo," he said gravely. "What a pity Troy was your model of Trevayne virtue for so long."

"He was the only one I knew, thanks to old grudges," she said on a note of accusation.

"Yes, perhaps we've all been at fault," he said wearily, then turned to Peregrine, who had lowered the boy to the ground and stood there, listening to the brief little exchanges with a curious expression.

"Are you crazy, Perry?" he said. "Or was it just a bit of unthinking horse-play?"

Peregrine flung back his head and laughed.

"Oh, belt up, Dom!" he said. "We were all brought up the hard way, and it didn't hurt us. The old man wouldn't have stood for any cry-baby nonsense, as you ought to know."

"Dad didn't make such a good job of us at that," his brother retorted. "Troy with his seductions, you very likely with yours, and I—"

"And what sort of scandal are you going to confess to, Big Brother? If you haven't gone wenching like the rest of us, you're no true son of Dad's! What brand's been left on you to prove the old boy's methods wrong?"

"A brand you wouldn't understand at all. Now clear off and let the boy come to me. It'll do no good to brawl here and frighten him further. I'll deal with you later. Let him come."

"If he will, but he hasn't shown much confidence in you so far, has he?" Peregrine jeered, and gave the child a little prod with the toe of his shoe.

Nicky was still sitting in a heap where he had been dropped at his uncle's feet, and had not moved. He was like a young bird frozen to the ground with fright, thought Laura, watching Dominic go down on one knee in the grass. Cleo made a sudden impatient movement towards her son as if she would pull him to his feet and end the uncomfortable scene, and Laura signalled her back. This was to be a testing time, she knew instinctively, not for the boy, but for Dominic who had never managed to break his brother's effortless spell.

"Come to me, Nicky," he said gently. "The dog's won't move unless I tell them to. Come, and I'll give you a piggy-back home."

The child just stared at him, but did not move, a hic-coughing sob the only reminder of his cruelly silenced screams.

"Come on. I'll be your unicorn and take you home safely."

"Playing unicorn is *my* privilege," said Peregrine with confident amusement. "Come to your Uncle Perry, Nicky, and make friends again." He stooped to toss the boy up to his shoulder, very sure of himself, and Nicky found his voice and his mobility at the same moment.

"No! No! Uncle Dom's my unimecorn for ever and ever!" he shouted, and ran across the grass and into Dominic's arms, where he burst into tears again.

"Well, what d'you know!" exclaimed Peregrine with quite genuine astonishment. "The dirty little turncoat! Come on, Cleo, let's go back to the house and have a drink—we're clearly not wanted here, and we can remove the dogs with us and leave the coast clear for tears and kisses. Laura? No? Well, perhaps not—she looks in need of tears and kisses, too."

Linking arms with Cleo, he sauntered off with a swagger, whistling the dogs after him. As they went, he flung a final taunt over his shoulder:

"Your score today, Big Brother—tomorrow I'll win him back. Be seeing you!"

CHAPTER EIGHT

LAURA lay back on the grass, allowing her attention to drift as the tension seeped out of her bones leaving them fluid and supine. She would have liked to lie where she was for ever in that blissful state of inertia, with her eyes closed, she thought, but when she felt a hand unexpectedly touch her forehead, she started up in fresh apprehension.

"Nicky?" she said, finding that Dominic was sitting beside her with an anxious look on his face.

"He's all right—he's playing over there quite happily. I gave him my handkerchief to turn him into a pirate," Dominic said and, sure enough, the boy was strutting round a gorse bush brandishing a stick, and with Dominic's handkerchief knotted round his neck as if nothing had happened.

"Aren't children ex-*extraordinary*!" said Laura, and wanted to laugh hysterically. Instead the tears came, those tears which earlier had refused stubbornly to flow and bring relief, and Dominic pulled her into his arms.

"Let it come," he said above her head. "It'll do you more good than the shot of brandy you ought to be having."

She wept with a child's unrestrained abandonment to tears, and he held her against him with the comforting reassurance of an old-fashioned nanny and said no more until she was quiet.

"I'm s-sorry," she gulped at last, accepting his offer of a handkerchief with gratitude, "I can't think why I had to do that now."

"Bit of delayed shock—quite common, and far the best way of getting rid of tension. Better now?"

"Yes, thank you—" She blew her nose violently, conscious of embarrassment. "I—I didn't mean to treat you to a scene, Dominic—you must have had enough for one day."

"But the Trevaynes thrive on scenes, I'm sure you must have noticed," he retorted. "Why should your own small indulgence embarrass you? You've cried on my shoulder before, the first time we met—remember?"

"It's not very tactful to remind me," she said. "Any shoulder would have done."

"Oh, I quite appreciated that; in fact, as I remember, you had mistaken me for the devil on that occasion, so you clearly weren't fussy as to whose shoulder you selected!"

He was, she supposed, only trying to rally her with his own peculiar brand of nonsense, but she wished he did not always have to treat her with that amused indulgence. As if he had guessed her thoughts he said in a different tone of voice:

"Don't mind my teasing, Laura. Sometimes it's a cover-up—the only defence I have."

"You said that to me once before."

"Did I?"

"That morning in the stable yard. You were excusing yourself, I think, for treating me like a child. I'm not a child, you know."

The arm about her tightened and she felt the hard roughness of his labourer's hands as they touched her face for a moment.

"No, you're not. But you're so *young*, Laura—so at the mercy of your own inexperience—so credulous in some ways. Sometimes I'm afraid of—" He broke off abruptly as if he was about to be trapped into saying too much, and she felt her colour begin to rise. Cleo's taunts and Peregrine's careless banter had only too probably been dropped in other quarters, she thought. Not sharing his brother's callousness in the matter of collecting scalps, he was trying to warn her that he had suspected that growing weakness and didn't want her to be hurt. It would account, of course, for his rather distant manner since Saturday.

"It's humiliating!" she burst out, reverting to the old habit of speaking her thoughts aloud, and pulled out of his comforting embrace.

"Your youth?" he said, his eyes tender, and she nodded quickly because it was the easiest way out.

"It's rather sad, you know, how one resents one's youth at a time when it should be so precious, and then, when it's gone, it's too late," he said.

"Too late? For what?"

"Oh, lots of things. Have I told you the story of the cuckoo of Zennor yet?"

"No."

"Zennor is a place in Cornwall, and the story goes that the villagers once built a hedge round a cuckoo to hold fast to the spring. Do you like the idea?"

"Yes," she said, "it's charming. Is there a parable in that, too, like the unicorn?"

"Perhaps. You were taken with that legend, weren't you? Nicky, I'm afraid, thought it a poor sort of story with a tame finish."

"I looked up about unicorns in a sort of old dictionary you have in the book-room."

"Did you, now? And what did you learn?"

"I have it by heart. 'The unicorn is a mythical and heraldic beast with the legs of a buck, the tail of a lion, the head and body of a horse and a single horn, and its eyes are blue . . .'" She broke off suddenly and sat staring at him; at the strong column of neck rising from the open shirt, the lips caught up by the scar in a one-sided smile of rather too comprehensive amusement, and finally the eyes which, against the dusky skin, looked vividly, startlingly blue.

"Coincidence, isn't it?" he said a little mockingly, and she lowered her own eyes and said hurriedly:

"Then, of course, the book goes on to tell the story and ends up, 'so he suffers himself to be captured' . . . don't you think that's a nice way of putting it? Are you the only Trevayne to have blue eyes, Dominic?"

"I believe so. That's my mother coming out in me. Talking of unicorns, it's time we took our young pirate home."

But Nicky was already with them, having caught the only word he understood of the conversation, and demanding: "Unimecorns! Unimecorns!" as Dominic got to his feet, clamoured to be taken up on his shoulder for the promised piggy-back.

Since the boy slowed his uncle's normally gruelling pace to a comfortable walk, Laura was able to keep up without running, and as they made their way over the young, springy turf that was beginning to cover the headland with fresh growth, Laura felt contentment rise again within her. It made no matter that the dark Trevayne must never know he had stolen her heart and closed the door on the last of childhood, for neither he nor anyone else, could take away her private dreams; they at least would be left to her when she had gone.

Nicky, delighted by such unaccountable behaviour in the sterner of his uncles. jigged up and down on his shoulders, and although. when they were met at the gates by the dogs which Peregrine had evidently failed to shut up, he clutched Dominic tightly round the neck and sat very still, he did not scream, or even whimper.

"That's the way," said his uncle cheerfully. "Brave as a lion, you must be, Dominic Trevayne. as I've always thought—did you know we had the same name? Tell you what. Nicky—we'll find you a puppy for your own, nice and small and fluffy Would you like that?"

"I might . . ." the boy replied doubtfully, but he was clearly impressed by being told he was as brave as a lion, for he said more firmly: "Would it be my very *own*?"

"Your very own, and no one shall look after it but you," Dominic said, setting him down at the open front door.

"Cleo wouldn't let me take it home," Nicky said, tentatively patting old Rowley, who shuffled across the hall to greet them, too stiff and blind now to exercise with the lurchers.

"Well you won't be going away for a long time," Dominic said briskly as they went into the hall Cleo, who had clearly been hanging about. waiting for them, linked an arm through his and said with a warm little sigh of relief:

"How *nice*! Penzion seems to be home to us, now, and London's not a good place for children. is it? And of *course* Nicky can keep his puppy while we're here. Dom I'm so bitterly sorry I didn't stop that lunacy of Perry's on the cliffs. I really did think shock tactics were the best cure. We're such a tough, roughneck family, aren't we? I didn't want Troy's son to let you down. Will you forgive my stupidity and take Nicky over on your own terms?"

She must, thought Laura, hovering awkwardly in the background, have rehearsed that little speech while she waited, for it came out so smoothly. Dominic, whatever his private thoughts, regarded her with an alert eye and said:

"What terms, Cleo?"

"Well, that's for you to say, isn't it?" she replied with a little laugh. "But you've clearly made a conquest, haven't you? My obstinate child has evidently at last seen the light, and appreciates his Uncle Dom for what he is, don't you, Nicky?"

"He's my unimecorn," Nicky replied, tugging possessively at his uncle's coat-tails.

"You see?" said Cleo. "However misplaced Perry's intentions were, they've at least done you a good turn."

"Have they?" Dominic said with a certain dry amusement. "Oh, well, Perry can win himself back into most people's good graces, if he tries. I'll most likely be back in the doghouse again tomorrow. Let's go and have a drink — Laura certainly needs one."

"Laura?" Cleo sounded surprised as if she had not even been aware of her cousin's presence, but she disengaged herself from Dominic and said remorsefully:

"Darling, I'd quite forgotten you. We must have given you a nasty turn with all that silly horse-play. I was forgetting you aren't yet used to the family's rather primitive ways. Come along and have that drink."

"No, thanks. I'd rather go up and have a wash," Laura said, and Dominic turned to look at her.

"Are you feeling all right, Laura?" he asked quickly. "I think you should have that drink, you know."

"I'm quite all right. I simply want to get clean and tidy before lunch," she said a little desperately, and Cleo, looking relieved that she could be sure of the next quarter of an hour or so to herself, said carelessly:

"Just as you like, darling, but if you're going upstairs you might as well take Nicky with you and dump him in the nursery till lunchtime."

"I don't think," Dominic said, beginning to make a move towards the tea-room, "Laura will want to be bothered with Nicky just now — he's earned a drink. anyway. Come along with us, old chap, and we'll find you some ginger pop."

He followed Cleo into the tea-room and Laura felt the tears sting her eyelids. He could not have intimated more plainly that he wished to be alone with Cleo.

Down in the day-room Dominic and Cleo ate their lunch in the customary hurried silence, broken only by the intermittent remarks of necessity. such as requests for salt and pepper, and a vague comment on the weather. Peregrine, Cleo said, hoping to start a profitable line of conversation, had taken himself off racing, and would probably end up in the pubs, but Dominic merely raised his eyebrows and enquired why she hadn't gone with him. Cleo, who had resisted the temptation in the hope of better rewards, felt unreasonably annoyed, but, remembering that mealtimes had never been favourable for the broaching of serious topics, she wisely held her tongue.

When they had finished, however. and he showed signs of going out of doors again, she said boldly:

"Don't you think it's time, Dom, that we had a serious talk and came down to brass tacks? We've been here over six weeks and we can't stay on indefinitely — at any rate, Laura can't."

For a moment he hesitated, then he gave a little shrug.

"Yes, perhaps it is, in view of this morning's rather unpleasant incident," he said. "Come into the book-room."

It didn't sound a very promising opening, and she said as she settled herself in a chair by the fire which, despite the warm weather, was still lighted every day:

"You remind me of a schoolmarm, darling. The only time you invite anyone into your holy of holies it's usually for a wigging."

He sat himself down behind his desk and smiled as she made a face at him.

"Force of habit," he said. "I work at this desk so it's natural to sit here. As for wiggings, someone must have been spinning you yarns. Perry's the only one I've ever found it necessary to blast, and that can happen anywhere."

"And Laura?"

"Laura? I've never had occasion to haul her over the coals — what on earth do you mean?"

She was quick to hear the unguarded note in his voice and said with a little shrug:

"Just an impression I get; I'm probably wrong, but you do scare her, you know. Mind you, some young girls, if their heads are still full of adolescent nonsense, rather enjoy being scared — providing it's followed up, of course, with a little soothing necking as consolation. Quite a common form of dalliance in both the sexes, I believe. Why are you looking at me like that, Dom? Is it your particular brand of necking?"

"No, it is not, and I find it hard to believe that you get that sort of impression from your cousin," he said, looking a little white and she shrugged again, this time with a graceful little suggestion of apology.

"Oh, well, perhaps I got it wrong," she said. "*I* wouldn't blame you for making a pass or two, darling, if Laura's type is to your liking, but *she* wouldn't understand. The poor sweet's terribly single-hearted where her affections are concerned, and they *are* rather fixed on Perry at the moment, as I told you. But let's forget about Laura and talk about Nicky. Have you any plans for him, or am I relying too much on your generosity?"

"Yes. I have plans," he said briskly. "I'd intended waiting a little longer before putting anything concrete before you, as I wanted to be sure the course of action I propose would be right for us both. You've shown me, however, that you take an adult view over most things in life, and aren't plagued by sentiment like many women, so I'll concede there's little more to be gained by further delay."

"Go on," she said a little breathlessly. "This course of action — if it's right for you, Dom, then it's right for me."

"I wonder. I wonder if my assessment of you is correct," he said, and she narrowed her eyes at him in open invitation.

"I'm sure it is — haven't you always prided yourself on your judgement? Even Perry admits you're very seldom wrong. Try me and see, darling — I think I know what you're going to say, anyway."

"Do you, Cleo? Well, that certainly makes things easier for both of us, though I hadn't listed you as a mind-reader in addition to your other abilities and charms."

"Well, Laura gave me the right clue," she said. "You wanted Nicky."

"Oh, I see. Yes, Cleo, I'd like to have the boy here under my own supervision. I want to give him a good start in life quite apart from any financial security. He has, you see, his father's blood to contend with when he's older, and Troy — forgive me — was not very stable."

"He has my blood, too," she countered quickly, and he smiled.

"But you, my very glamourous sister-in-law, would be the first to admit, I'm sure, that you're not at all fitted to bring up a headstrong boy."

"Not alone," she said. "I've never pretended to be a good mother, I just haven't got a clue — but with a man beside me strong enough to take a father's place and keep us both in order, it might be another story."

He reached for his pipe and began to fill it from the tobacco jar at his elbow.

"I agree, but that's a little chancy, isn't it?" he said. "You must, and will, undoubtedly marry again, my dear, but a child, I know, can be a handicap to remarriage these days when the average decent young chap one's likely to meet isn't over-blessed with this world's goods. If I took Nicky off your hands, you would be completely free."

"What on earth are you getting at?" she asked, and

134

at the change in her voice he looked across at her, frowning.

"But I thought you understood," he said. "I'm proposing, if you are willing, to provide entirely for the boy, so long as he can be brought up here, with the appropriate schooling, of course, when the time comes. I don't suggest adoption unless you wish it, as I'd want you to feel free to see him at any time and keep in touch with all of us. If you marry, as of course you will, you can have him to stay if you want, but you can feel yourself free of all responsibility, both financial and moral. What's the matter, Cleo? I thought you'd jump at the offer — you never wanted the child, did you?"

"And did Laura tell you that one — among other charming little tittle-tattles, I don't doubt?" she spat at him, and he looked at her gravely.

"Laura has nothing to do with this, and we'll leave her out of this discussion, if you please," he said. "I'm well aware of your physical attractions, Cleo, but I'm aware, too, that your failings, unfortunately, are almost identical with Troy's, and that's not a good heritage for Nicky."

There was a long silence between them and he watched her curiously, assessing the changing conflicts revealed in her face; bitter chagrin, greed, temper, and finally spite. She looked in that moment, he thought, very like Troy had looked when crossed, as Nicky was beginning to look already.

"It's Laura, isn't it?" she said with a hard little laugh. "My sly little cousin's made good use of her time here, and you've been caught, haven't you?"

"I don't think I understand you, Cleo," he said patiently.

"I think you do," she snapped. "Perry was right when he said you were the protective type. You've fallen for Laura's milk-and-water charms, haven't you? The predatory overlord condescending to the humble admirer — but it's Perry who's the favoured one, don't forget; it's Perry your ewe lamb would like to bed down with, and probably has, for all I know."

He brought his fist crashing down on the desk with a suddenness that startled her, and some of the spleen began to seep out of her as she met his furious eyes.

"When you've quite done with this very distasteful display of vulgarity, Cleo, we'll try to talk business, for I fancy it's the only subject on which you and I are likely to agree," he said. "What inducement do you want to give up the boy?"

She began to fidget, torn between a desire to hit out at him further, and an instinct to cash in on what remained to her.

"Why should I give up my own child to satisfy Trevayne pride in the future?" she said, controlling her voice to a semblance of its old husky drawl. "Besides, it shouldn't be necessary. I'd thought — evidently mistakenly — that you and I between us could have handled that little problem very neatly."

"Yes?" he said, and waited.

"You devil, Dom! You must know quite well what's been in my mind! Am I so unattractive to you, or am I not good enough for the head of the house of Trevayne?" she said.

His eyes softened momentarily to a faint touch of pity, not for the hurt and sense of rejection another woman might have felt, but for the humiliation that might torment her later, and when he answered, his voice was more gentle.

"Cleo, let's not go into personalities which can only prove painful to us both," he said. "If I've misled you in any way, I must beg your pardon, but whatever brash notion you may have had of killing two birds with one stone, it wouldn't have worked you know."

"Why? I speak your language, don't I?"

"You speak Trevayne language, as I told you once before. It's not necessarily the same as mine. Now, if you'd like to sit down again, we'll discuss this thing on a purely commercial basis. In addition to my original proposals, I'm prepared to make you a generous allowance, since I understand most of your parents' money went in keeping you and Troy. I'm not ungrateful for your loyalty to Troy, and you can name your own sum within reason."

She did not sit down, but leant against the desk, mistress of herself again, and smilingly casual.

"Oh, no," she said. "I have my terms, too. I want marriage."

He got up himself, and idly rearranged some papers on the desk, intimating that he wished the interview over.

"You wouldn't, I assure you, Cleo, care about being married to me," he said with infuriating composure. "You force me to speak plainly, but — I wouldn't take at all kindly to being cuckold in my own house, and that's what you had in mind, wasn't it?"

She slapped him hard across the cheek, and had the momentary satisfaction of seeing the scar stand out in angry relief against his skin before he leaned across the desk and caught her wrists and held them, as he had done that night at supper.

"You'll do that once too often, my dear," he rapped out at her, and there was at last a hint of breaking control in his voice. "You're more naïve than I thought you, Cleo, if you imagined I was unaware that you and Perry were having an affair. It was no concern of mine, since you're both adult and well-matched in that respect, but it scarcely commended you to me as a possible wife. Now, go away and think things over quietly. When you have your sense of proportion back, let me know and we'll talk again."

He let her go and she stood rubbing her bruised wrists, and looking a little frightened.

"Very well, Dom," she said at last. "I'll do just that, but don't think I can be bought off so easily. Don't forget, either, that whatever favours I've had from Perry, Laura has shared them . . . It must feel like old times with Perry charming your girl away, just as Troy did . . . You would seem, my dear brother-in-law, to be one of these unfortunate characters who are doomed to be passed over. Tomorrow, I don't mind betting, Perry will have won back Nicky again." It was, she congratulated herself, a good exit line, and judging by Dominic's expression, one that went home. She turned her back on him, carelessly flicked the neat pile of papers on to the floor, and sauntered out of the room.

Laura found her later crying hysterically on her bed and throwing any object within reach across the room. These crying bouts, once so alarming, no longer frightened Laura, who had found that, providing one did not make the mistake of proffering comfort in the normal way, the fit would wear itself out and Cleo emerge very much refreshed by her loss of control. So she stood now, waiting and saying nothing, wondering what Dominic could have said to upset her.

"Was — was Dominic hard on you — about Nicky, I mean?" Laura asked, feeling the moment had arrived for tactful sympathy, but the venomous look her cousin suddenly bestowed on her gave her the sensation of being slapped.

"Hard on me!" she exclaimed. "What do you think I am — an awed schoolgirl to be reduced to tears by a few cross words from the beloved! Is that the effect he has on you, sly, simple Laura? Because he *is* the beloved, isn't he? I was watching your face up there on the cliffs, and you gave yourself away."

Laura's mouth quivered, but she replied with dignity.

"What I may or may not feel for Dominic is my own affair and need embarrass nobody."

"Well, you've embarrassed Dom, my ostrich-like child. He couldn't fail to see, any more than I could, the sickly symptoms bursting out all over you. He feels you must have mistaken ordinary civility for encouragement, and asked me to drop you a hint, as a matter of fact."

"Is that," enquired Laura with admirable self-possession, "what you were crying about?" But although she had the rather hollow satisfaction of seeing the chagrin in her cousin's face, there was a cold, heavy lump in her heart. Had she not thought that Dominic himself had been trying to warn her up there on the headland?

"No, it's not," snapped Cleo, answering the question with acute dislike in her voice. "I happen to have a splitting headache and feel rather sick."

138

"Bilious, I shouldn't wonder. Too many chocolates," said Laura, and Cleo threw a pillow at her.

"You seem very full of yourself of late," she said waspishly. "Don't let wishful thinking about Dom's non-existent intentions turn your head completely, darling. He has quite other ideas, I assure you. Incidentally, he thinks it's time you went home."

"Did he say so?"

"Not in so many words, but the inference was obvious. He's naturally sorry you've rather lost your heart, and thinks it would be better if you went away."

"I see. And what about you? Have you settled Nicky's affairs?"

"Oh, yes, that little problem is working out very nicely. We shall be stopping on, of course."

"I see," said Laura again, and Cleo smiled like a cat full of cream.

"I'm sure you do, darling. Well — have a little think about it and make your plans. You'll find Dom will be quite generous when you do go."

"What on earth do you mean?"

"Well, you evidently went bleating to him that I didn't pay you for looking after Nicky, which wasn't very nice of you, was it?"

For an instant Laura was bewildered. That morning when Dominic had casually questioned her regarding that misleading designation of her position among them seemed so long ago that she had forgotten.

"Oh, don't be silly," she said as recollection came back. "I explained that you and I had never been on those sort of terms, and I thought he understood."

"He understood, no doubt, exactly what you intended him to," said Cleo, getting off the bed and starting to repair the damage to her face. "Anyway, he means to make it up to you when you leave."

"Make it up to me? How?"

"A nice little bonus for services rendered, I imagine — the same as any other privileged employee."

"Thank you for warning me," Laura said bleakly. "Nothing would induce me to take money from Dom-

139

inic. For one thing he owes me nothing, and for another—"

"For another your poor little pride would have a horrid set-down being obliged to accept a tip from the master — I know," said Cleo, who, with that astonishing gift she possessed for rapid recuperation, now seemed completely restored. Whatever the cause for that outburst of crying, it had certainly not been a headache, thought Laura, and got out of the room as quickly as she could for fear she should succumb to tears herself. She would, of course, she thought disgustedly, have to meet Dominic at the bottom of the stairs.

"Oh, Laura," he said as she came to an abrupt halt, "can you spare me a moment?"

She had been going to seek solace outside in the cool spring breeze on the headland, but much as she wished to avoid him, it was scarcely possible to refuse. She followed him into the book-room, wondering whether he was going to suggest, himself, that it was time she left Penzion, and was not reassured when he asked:

"What are your future plans, Laura? Have you a job to go back to?"

"Not at the moment," she replied.

"So you're free of commitments as far as employers are concerned?"

"Oh, yes. My last employers went bust. Flower shops tend to, you know."

"Do they? Good. Well then, I have a proposition for you. Would you stay on here?"

She looked at him blankly. Whatever she had expected to hear him say it was certainly not this.

"What do you mean?" she said, and taking a quick surreptitious glance at his face, thought he looked tired; tired and rather alarmingly austere.

"Exactly what I say. If, as you have suggested to me before, you have enough liking for Penzion to want to stay with us, I have a proposition that might appeal to you. I'd like you to stay on, if you will, for Nicky, until I can make more settled plans."

"You wish to employ me as a nanny?" she said

with such an absurd imitation of a correct prospective applicant that he looked at her in surprise.

"Good God, no! That is — well, I'd like you to stop on just as you are now — as my guest," he said, and for the first time in her knowledge of him, sounded a little uncertain of himself.

"I was given to understand," she said, "that you thought it was time I left."

"Who gave you that idea — Cleo?" he asked.

"It's an idea I've had myself," she replied evasively. "I only came here in the first place to help Cleo out, and I've my own life to lead, haven't I?"

"And what are you going to do with your life, might one ask, Miss Mouse?" he said with such an avuncular air of indulgence that she whipped round on her stool to confront him.

"I'm getting a little tired of this mode of address, Dominic," she said. "I may seem like a child to you, but I've been earning my own living for the past two years, and that does give one some knowledge of adult affairs, you know."

The teasing amusement left his face and he regarded her gravely.

"I'm sorry," he said, sounding stiff and awkward. "I'm going about this the wrong way, I'm afraid. I wasn't disparaging your capabilities — or your much despised youth, or your acquaintance with adult affairs. I think I need you, Laura."

He said it quite humbly and with a hint of surprise, as if he had only just convinced himself, and Laura, battling with so many conflicting emotions, felt her bones melting again, as they had that morning on the headland.

"What do you want of me?" she asked a little helplessly, and he replied with abrupt ambiguity:

"What you can't give me, probably. Will you stay?"

"If Cleo has agreed to your plans for Nicky, there's no need, surely?" she said gently, and his sudden frown was not very pleasant.

"Have you seen your cousin since lunch?" he asked.

"Yes. She seemed rather upset."

"Very likely. Didn't she explain?"

"About what?"

He made a little gesture of impatience.

"Why all this fencing with me, Laura? I asked you a perfectly straightforward question."

"It's you who do the fencing, I think," she said. "I really don't know what you're getting at."

"Don't or won't?" he countered, and she gave a little evasive shrug.

"Very well," he said. "I'll put my question another way. What did your cousin tell you?"

"About your plans for Nicky? Only that they were working out very nicely and she would be stopping on."

"I see. And how was she proposing to cope with the boy?"

"I didn't ask. Bella could manage for a time, I suppose."

"You don't really want to stay, do you?" he said, his voice sounding a little harsh. "Perhaps I was wrong to think you were happy here. Is it Perry you want to get away from?"

"Perry? No — oh, no! He makes things easier for me."

"Yes, I see. In that case, a few more weeks of his company shouldn't hurt you, should it? You might even turn it to advantage if you don't give up and run away." He spoke with such a savage bitterness that she was bewildered.

"I don't know what you're getting at," she said again, getting to her feet and shaking the creases from her skirt, hoping to end this very confusing interview, but he got to his own feet, hesitated a moment, then took a swift stride round the desk and took her by the shoulders.

"For God's sake, Laura, what's happened to you?" he exclaimed. "All the week-end you've been ill at ease with me — evasive. I don't seem to get through to you."

He had told her he thought he needed her, but it was, she knew now, only the need of a rather lonely man who, despite himself, had come to have a little fondness for an undemanding child. It wasn't

142

fair, she thought, to trade on the suspicion of her own feeling for him.

"You don't make it very easy," she said, then added, with the vague idea that a familiar absurdity might coax him away from more serious introspection, "Predatory overlords sit up on pedestals, you see."

His hands slipped from her shoulders to her wrists, with so painful a pressure that she cried out, and he was suddenly kissing her with Peregrine's familiar roughness.

She could do no more than submit and remain passive, for his grip on her wrists was so rigid, and his mouth so hard and demanding that response was impossible. She could not free her hands to slip them round his neck, as she would have liked, and when he let her go, abruptly, and with a suggestion of self-disgust, she still stood there, pliant and unprotesting.

"I'm sorry," he said, turning away. "You drove me to extremes, I'm afraid, ganging up like the others."

"Ganging up?" She touched her bruised lips tenderly, but her eyes were puzzled rather than shocked, and he drove his hands with an angry thrust into his trouser pockets.

"You and Perry. The predatory overlord is a dig that's begun to pall," he said, and she experienced a little surge of tenderness for him that he could be hurt by such foolish nonsense.

"I'm sorry," she said gently. "I just didn't understand you — and I've never ganged up on you, Dominic."

"No, of course you haven't," he said. "Do I apologise for my rough handling?"

"If I said predatory overlords never apologise, I suppose you would take it as another dig," she replied, and he gave her a quick, reluctant smile.

"Am I making a fool of myself?" he said, then with the abrupt change of mood which seemed to come to him so easily, added in quite a different tone of voice: "You haven't given me an answer."

"An answer?"

"To my proposition."

"You're full of propositions. Haven't you just made one to Cleo?" she said.

"You know my plans for Nicky," he replied rather impatiently. "Your cousin, when she's had time for second thoughts, may think them worth considering. In the meantime—" He broke off for a moment and she waited incuriously for him to continue, knowing the answer to this one. Cleo, of course, was keeping him guessing in the traditional manner; had she not said, only just now, that her plans were working out very nicely?

"In the meantime," he went on without noticing Laura's attention had wandered, "I'm most anxious the boy should have no disturbing indication of any change. If you leave too soon, his sense of security will be gone, so isn't it reasonable to ask you to put your own affairs aside, just for a little while?"

"*Reasonable!* Do you think reason has anything to do with Trevayne demands?" she exclaimed with a sudden revulsion of feeling.

He must have sensed the withdrawal behind her little spurt of indignation, for he said placatingly:

"Have I got off on the wrong foot again? I only meant that the boy is fond of you and wouldn't take kindly to losing his Moo-moo. If it's a question of money, Laura, which of course I should have thought of before, I will naturally see that you have an adequate salary."

"And a generous bonus at the end?" she said tartly, remembering Cleo's words, and he failed to catch the rising inflection in her voice.

"Certainly, if that's what you would expect," he replied with sudden stiffness. "I quite understand that you have a living to earn, and your cousin has already taken up too much of your time without any payment. Naturally, if you agree to stop on with us, I will see that you're not out of pocket."

It was too much, thought Laura, feeling that rarely indulged temper of hers rising in a spiral inside her.

"I wouldn't," she said, beginning to speak with such unfamiliar shrillness that he gave her a sharp look of attention, "accept a penny from you — not if I were *starving!* Cleo warned me you had this in mind — a generous bonus for a privileged employee, she said — a discreet settlement for services rendered which closes the book and puts everything on a comfortable, commercial footing. If you — if you dare hand me a cheque when I leave, Dominic Trevayne, I'll tear it up and — and I'll spit in your eye!"

She began to cry, and he took a quick step towards her, and would have taken her in his arms if she hadn't backed away.

"Laura, my dear — I've been clumsy — I had no idea of hurting you," he said, and his voice was the dark voice she had once so fancifully assigned to him, a voice which, at any other moment, would have proved her undoing. "What the hell has that damnable cousin of yours been saying?"

"Only what's true — only what you've just said yourself," she cried, not even pausing to consider whether "damnable" wasn't rather an odd way of alluding to one's future wife. "If I stay at all, it will be for Nicky's sake and his alone, and you can keep your money — you don't owe me anything — but I don't think I will — stay, I mean. I've had enough of being pushed around with no thought — *no thought at all,* I may tell you, that I have private feelings — yes, and private silly dreams, too, of my own."

"Oh, God damn it! Why in hell did you have to go and lose your stupid little heart to—" he began violently as she turned to make her escape, and as if on cue, the door opened noisily and Peregrine stood there, regarding them both with a very merry eye.

"What — *ho!*" he said, catching Laura as she bumped blindly into him. "Did I interrupt a tender moment? But no, the girl weeps — serves you right, you fickle jade, transferring your favours as soon as my back's turned! There's women for you, Dom!"

"Take your hands off her and get out; you're drunk!" snapped Dominic, but Laura clung to Peregrine, saying: "Take me away, Perry . . . take me away out of this house . . ."

"With pleasure, my pretty — we'll nip down to the local and have a cosy little get-together in the bar parlour. That will soon revive your flagging interest in me," Peregrine said, and with a knowing wink at his brother, put a firm arm round her and led her from the room.

"Do you think I'm drunk, Miss Bread-and-butter?" he enquired of Laura, rocking backwards and forward on the balls of his feet while he watched her with interest She had stopped to cool her burning forehead against the cold bronze of the unicorn, and he observed with curiosity how her fingers began exploring the model's outlines, running with loving tenderness over the arching neck and tapering horn.

"I wouldn't know," she said indifferently, trying not to sniff. "I thought you were going racing."

"So I did, but I left before the last race, and the pubs not being open yet, had never a stop on the way."

She smiled, beginning to regain her self-possession in the earthy comfort of his familiar line of bravado.

"I bet you saw more of the beer-tents than the horses," she said. "Why are you back so early? We thought you'd be sure to make a night of it."

"Call it curiosity — or maybe a slight sense of guilt, if you like. I wanted a word with the fascinating widow, as a matter of fact. Felt I'd rather left her holding the can after this morning's little display of fireworks. Did she get the rough side of Dom's tongue?"

"Maybe at first — she did seem in a bit of a state, only—"

"Only the clever puss turned it all to her advantage and winkled Dom's future plans out of him?"

"Yes, I think so."

"And you gleaned, dear Cousin Laura—"

"Only that she said her schemes were working out very nicely and she thought it was time I went home."

"Did she now? And was Brother Dom expressing the same view — thus causing tears and high words?"

"No, he wants me to stay — until he and Cleo marry, I presumed."

"O-ho . . . did Dom mention marriage, might one ask?"

"Nobody ever comes out with anything definite in this house, I've come to the conclusion," she exclaimed, and pressed a hand so violently down on the unicorn's horn that its tip pierced the skin. She stood staring down at the little bubble of blood welling up from the wound, and Peregrine said with a rather wicked glint in his eye:

"Now you've done it! The beast of the house has put his mark on you and you're caught!"

"It's the unicorn that has to be caught," she corrected him with faint reproof, and he grinned.

"So it is. Well, you'd better clean it up — those perishing trophies and phony antiques must be hatching with germs — I don't suppose anyone ever dusts them. How's the kid? None the worse for his fright, I hope?"

"Nicky?" She caught the handkerchief he tossed to her and alternately dabbed at the little wound and her own tear-stained face. "He's all right. He recovered very quickly with gentle handling."

"The healing touch of the head of the family proving itself superior in the end, one takes it," he said on the old jeering note of resentment, and Laura looked up.

"Why don't you leave the boy alone now?" she said, quickly. "You've had your fun at Dominic's expense; give him a chance now to follow up today's advantage. He really cares, you know, and you don't."

He looked at her serious face bent again over her hand. A thin shaft of sunlight caught unexpected gleams in the mousy hair and in the bronze of the unicorn outlined behind her head.

"Go and do something about your face and meet me down here in half an hour or so, and we'll nip down to the pub for a quick one," he said. "I want a word with Cousin Cleo, so that'll give you time to repair the ravages that my dear brother seems to have left on you. Stick a piece of Elastoplast on that hand — be seeing you!"

He went up the stairs, two at a time, and pausing at the head to look down, saw her still standing there, her back to the unicorn, looking down absently at her bandaged hand.

"Silly coot!" he muttered, and turned the handle of Cleo's door.

She was still sitting at the dressing-table where Laura had left her, putting the finishing touches to her face, and he stood behind her, pulling her back against him.

"Hullo, sweetie . . . Brother Dom torn a strip off you?" he said, rubbing his chin along her hair.

She gave a small, cross shrug as he touched her, then relaxed against him.

"On account of your nice little display this morning?" she replied. "No, curiously he didn't. Who would have suspected Dom of softness?"

"Haven't you yet got on to the pariah streak in Big Brother? Softness — or perhaps it would be more polite to call it tenderness — is Dom's pariah streak. That's why he's not for you, my pretty — far better make do with what you've got."

"But what I've got doesn't include what I want," she said.

"Is marriage so important? You're thoroughly amoral, darling, as you've often admitted, so why should you care?"

"Because," she said, "even today it's easier to get by with one's passions lawfully sanctioned. I'm not prepared to live furtively, even for you, darling."

"But you're prepared to carry on the affair if someone else gives you the protection of marriage?"

She turned to give him a curious look.

"Well, weren't you?" she said, and was genuinely surprised by the lack of immediate agreement in him.

"Yes, I suppose I was," he replied, sitting down on the bed and allowing himself to sprawl. "But some things tend to stick in the gullet, you know — even mine. Do I take it, then, that you've brought Dom up to scratch? No, I can see by your face you haven't. What, might one ask, did Big Brother's proposition amount to, then? Not the expected offer of marriage, I take it."

For a moment she was tempted to spill the whole

148

humiliating story, admitting her premature bungling of the affair, but Perry, though he undoubtedly wanted her for himself, wasn't to be trusted not to make mischief should it suit his book, so she replied quite calmly:

"He suggests that I hand over Nicky to him, in return for which he will make me an allowance at my own price."

"Well, what d'you know! Why the hell quibble about a little thing like marriage? Jump right in and grab your opportunity with both hands," he exclaimed, rolling over on the bed.

"Oh, no, if Big Brother wants Nicky he's going to have to pay for him in more than hard cash."

"Meaning?"

She shrugged, and he added slyly, "The little cousin, of course. Well, remember unicorns, my dear."

"Oh, really, Perry! That crummy old legend!"

"Well, what had *you* in mind, then? There's a bit of truth in these old legends, you know, and young virgins are very delectable bait."

"As you've already discovered, perhaps?"

"Not with the chaste Miss Bread-and-butter, my sweet, delightful though I find her in small doses."

"Dom's scarcely going to believe that, knowing your reputation, is he? He already thinks it's you who's stolen her innocent heart. I've worked on that one."

"You're full of spite, aren't you?" he remarked conversationally, then suddenly abandoned his casual air of inconsequence. "Don't be a damn fool, Cleo! You don't want the kid, and you don't really care about Dom — or Laura. If you can soak him for a decent settlement and no strings attached, cash in while the going's good. I might even play along, if he makes it worth my while. Anyway, don't antagonise him just for a bit of spleen."

"Spleen . . . spite . . . Troy taught me that very early," she said with a rather strange air of pride. "Yes, Perry, like you, I'm full of spite when I'm crossed. I *am* a Trevayne now."

"Like all converts you're more fervent than those

149

born into their faith," he said, getting off the bed and patting the creases from his clothes, then he suddenly fell back on it again, pulling her with him.

"Stop needling me, you little bitch," he said, his mouth on hers. "You know you've got me, just as you got Troy . . . there were times when you almost got me to the altar until you had larger ideas. Chuck it up, Cleo . . . make your little killing work for us both . . ."

"And what does that mean?" she asked, without really caring, as she felt the familiar touch of his hands on her breasts, her limbs, and knew her own animal attraction reaching out to his.

"Never mind . . . never mind . . ." he murmured, and just for a moment, as his lips and his body made demands, she was suddenly a young girl again, wanting the innocent, sweeter things of love, seeking assurance of her own capacity for giving.

After he had gone, she lay for a long time drifting back into the half-remembered hopes and uncertainties of late adolescence, then, realising the hour was growing late, and with Perry and Laura safely out of the way Dominic was vulnerable to a flank attack, she renewed what items of make-up Perry had ruined and went downstairs.

Peregrine drove Laura through empty lanes, and villages shuttered and deserted by the Bank Holiday exodus to the towns, already regretting his impetuous invitation. Fresh as he was from Cleo's experienced hands, the negative little cousin seemed no fit companion for an evening's jollification in the pub, though it might be both entertaining and instructive to see how many drinks it would take to get Miss Laura Smith to let her back hair down.

Laura, on the other hand, was experiencing a blessed sense of relief as the car took them away from Penzion and she felt the cool wind in her hair and saw the young spring sky arching above them. It was a pity, she thought, when they arrived all too soon at St. Mewan, to spend such a fine evening in the stuffy bar parlour of a pub, but at least it sounded cheerful with the noise and laughter coming from the public bar next door.

Conversation was desultory at first, for Peregrine seemed silent and morose, though more likely, Laura thought, with her practical acceptance of other people's moods, it was all the beer he had consumed at the races now lying heavy on his stomach.

"I don't want to be involved," she said suddenly with that precipitate habit she had of voicing her thoughts, and Peregrine raised an enquiring eyebrow, reminding her of the impression of horns she had had on the train.

"Involved in what?" he asked. "Drink?"

"Whatever's going on at Penzion."

"But you *are* involved, my sweet, aren't you? You've lost your silly little heart to Dom, and he — well, your guess is as good as mine."

"But you know, don't you, Perry."

"Well, if I do, I'm not telling. I thought you said you didn't want to be involved."

She sighed and he told her to drink up and drown her sorrows.

"We're both drowning our sorrows, aren't we?" she said, mournfully. "There's something I want to ask you, Perry."

It was dark in the little back parlour and her face was in shadow, but he found the innocent column of her slender neck, and her pale, fluttering hands oddly touching.

"Well, ask away. What's scaring you?" he said.

"I'm not scared," she said, "just a little nervous because I'm going to be impertinent."

"Are you, now?"

"Yes. Look, Perry, I know you and Cleo are having an affair and that's none of my business, but — but I want to know if — if Cleo marries Dominic, are you really going on with it?"

"Well for crying out loud!" he exclaimed, swallowing his drink at a gulp. "What the hell's that got to do with you?"

He crossed to the hatch a little unsteadily, not waiting for a reply, but when he came back with the drinks she answered politely:

"It's got to do with me because I care. I care, I mean, that Dominic has a square deal. Cleo doesn't, you see."

"Now look here," he blustered, beginning to sound a little slurred, "you can't go asking indecent questions like that. What do you suppose your more civilised cousin would say to such notions?"

"What she's already said — that she means to have her cake and eat it. Cleo is ruthless, you know. But you, Perry — I don't really believe that even you—" She had clasped her hands in an unconscious little gesture of entreaty, stilling their restless movement, and leaned towards him across the table between them.

He leaned forward himself across the table to peer more closely into her face, and put out a hand to touch her, seeking assurance for something already forgotten, and she suddenly smiled at him, the trusting but slightly mischievous smile of a little girl begging a favour.

It was only then that he became aware of the unnatural silence which, for several minutes, had fallen upon the bar next door, and he turned uneasily to glance across the half open door, mentally cursing any interruption at this rewarding moment.

Dominic stood there, a glass in his hand, regarding them with such an expression of bitter darkness that Laura, following the direction of Peregrine's eyes, gave an involuntary little cry and then sat very still.

CHAPTER NINE

TO LAURA he looked, silhouetted against the bright light behind him, as he had that first night on the station platform; the dark stranger who had seemed like an apparition owing to both piratical forebears and ancestry of a more sinister origin. Then he closed the door behind him, shutting out the background of light, and the illusion was lost.

"Are you ready to come home?" he said with casual enquiry, and to Laura, who had almost expected his first words to be accompanied by the smell of smoke and brimstone, the question seemed an anticlimax.

"Yes," she said a little nervously. Peregrine might be too full of dutch courage to notice the danger signals, but she could see them, and it wouldn't take much, she thought, to start one of their brawls. "Come on, Perry — it's been a nice party, but I'm getting hungry."

"Sit down, Miss Bread-and-butter. When I bring you out for an evening's mild entertainment, you'll go when I'm ready."

Laura sat down, not from any conscious obedience to his command but because her legs felt weak.

"You see?" he said with triumphant insolence. "Aren't you rather overdoing the rôle of watchdog, Big Brother? Your ewe lamb's scarcely under age for licensed premises, so why spoil the fun?"

Dominic's eyes went from the rows of empty glasses to Laura's embarrassed face, and he observed quite mildly:

"If your idea of fun is to get a girl who's unused to liquor tight, then I think interference is necessary. What were you hoping for — an easy roll in the hay on the way home?"

Peregrine got to his feet unsteadily, an angry flush on his dark face.

"If that's the way you want it, Dom, come outside

and take a licking. You haven't much luck with the girls you pick to defend, have you?"

His brother caught him a blow across the cheek which sent him reeling back to his seat, but he did not, as Laura feared, hit back, but sat, glowering and sullen and more than a little fuddled.

"You'll be sorry for that — you'll be very sorry," he said thickly, but Dominic took no further notice of him. The violence with which he had sat down had upset glasses and plant alike on the table, and Laura's hidden cache was revealed, spilling their untasted contents in little trickles over the cloth.

For the first time Dominic's face relaxed in a rather grim smile and he turned to Laura, now on her feet again.

"I misjudged you, Miss Mouse," he said. "It would appear it was you trying to get my brother sloshed, not the other way about, and apparently succeeding very ably. Shall we go? We'll leave Perry to follow at his leisure."

He emptied his own glass without hurry, set it down on the table with the others, then opened the door for Laura to precede him into the street.

"Well!" she said, getting into the car parked beside Peregrine's. "I must say my sympathies are rather with Perry."

"That, of course, is taken as read, judging by your expression when I so inconveniently interrupted," he replied as he took his seat beside her. "Was the affair coming along nicely?"

"I don't know what you mean," she said, flushing.

"Don't you? Weren't you trying softening-up tactics?"

"Yes, I was, and thanks to you, I still haven't had my answer," she said crossly, not understanding in the least what he might be hinting at, and his answering smile was not at all reassuring.

"Your cousin's more experienced methods don't become you," he said, starting up the engine.

She sensed disparagement in this remark, and said resentfully:

"What's Cleo got to do with it?"

"I might make a guess, but you probably wouldn't care to be told you were making rather a poor hand at taking a leaf out of her book," he said. "She had a pretty shrewd idea what you were up to, you know, and felt she might have given you bad advice."

"Is that why you came?" she said as the car moved slowly down the deserted street. "Did she send you to rescue me from a fate worse than death, or some such corny nonsense?"

"Oh, I hardly think you would have come to much harm in the local where we're all well known, apart from a possible thick head in the morning — though of course it's Perry who's going to have the thick head as it turns out," he said, reverting to his old manner of dealing with ill-considered absurdities, but her little spurt of indignation died as she remembered his contemptuous remark to his brother. *An easy roll in the hay on the way home . . .* was that what he thought of her? Had his intervention been merely a self-imposed duty as head of the house to save a silly young girl from making a fool of herself?

He did not break the stony silence between them, neither did he hurry through the lanes and villages as Peregrine had, and when they came to the cliff road which led to Penzion, he pulled up on the verge and cut his engine.

"We might as well enjoy the last of the sunset," he remarked as though nothing less trivial lay between them than a Bank Holiday outing in fine weather. "We get some spectacular sunsets in these parts, you know."

"Do you?" she said politely, and he turned to look at her, settling himself sideways behind the wheel and resting an arm along the back of the seat.

"You're tired, aren't you?" he said . . . Yes, she was tired, desperately tired, and the little wound in her hand was beginning to throb. She had managed to fight back the tears which had threatened earlier, but it would not take much, she thought, to bring them back, and of all else she wished to preserve the last of her dignity.

"Well it's been quite a day," she replied with a

155

gallant attempt at lightness. "Scenes . . . assaults . . . high words . . . tantrums . . . the Trevaynes take these things as a matter of course."

"Not all of them — but you mentioned assaults," he said with the lift of an eyebrow, and she said, resisting evasion:

"Well, you did pounce on me in the book-room — certainly more in the nature of an assault than a tender embrace, I would have said — unprovoked, too."

He smiled, and in the gathering darkness his face seemed to soften to the old half-impatient indulgence.

"If there's one thing more than another I admire about you, Miss Mouse, it's that brash refusal to parley with the enemy," he said. "I apologise for my assault, as you call it, but it was not unprovoked."

"N-not?"

"No. I didn't at all care for your adoption of my brother's not very complimentary epithet for me — even though it was meant as a joke."

"Then I apologise, too," she said handsomely. "Only—"

"Only what?"

"It — well, it seems an odd reaction if one's annoyed with somebody."

"Yes, I daresay. You don't understand very much about the way a man's emotions react, do you?"

"No," she said humbly, "and you least of all, Dominic. You — you alternate so quickly between aloof withdrawal and a sort of indulgent tolerance. It's very confusing."

"Indulgent tolerance . . . is that all you think I've felt for you?"

"Did that sound unimportant to you?" she asked, resting her head against his arm with the natural confidence of a young child. "It wasn't to me, you see, because I know — Cleo's often told me — how irritating I can be with my naïve remarks and what she calls whimsies. You may have laughed at me kindly, but you always listened."

He was silent for such a long minute that she turned her head to look at him, wondering if she had, as so often, given the wrong answer. He was looking down at her with such an unexpected expression of pain that she put out a hand to touch his face.

"Am I being naïve again?" she asked a little anxiously, and he smiled at her.

"No, my dear, just rather naturally uncomprehending," he answered. "Do you remember we once talked of defences — a cover-up for more serious thoughts and, possibly, emotions? You didn't understand, did you? I left it too long, it seems."

"I have defences too, you know — I suppose everyone has. Covering up isn't always easy, either," she said, remembering that Cleo had told her she could be an embarrassment to him; and he, thinking of Peregrine who took so easily and cared so little, answered gently: "No, it isn't. What have you done to your hand?"

It was the bandaged hand she had put out to touch him and he captured it as she was about to withdraw it.

"I pricked it on the unicorn's horn," she said indifferently, and he gave her an odd look.

"H'm . . . quite a nasty little wound, and looking rather angry. Does it hurt?"

"It throbs a bit."

"It would seem the superstition's working the wrong way round — the wretched creature's succeeded in administering the poison instead of the antidote. That'll larn you not to muck about with unicorns," he said, and began binding up her hand again with a clean handkerchief of his own.

"Perry said the beast of the house had put its mark on me and I was caught," she said sleepily, enjoying the excuse for having him touch her, but winced as he tightened the final knot with an unexpected jerk. "I told him, of course, it was the unicorn that has to be captured, not the maiden."

"Don't you be too sure. Either way, you'd be advised to leave the chancy brutes alone until the time is ripe."

"Are they chancy?"

"Very! Proud and rebellious and defiant, too, according to Spenser."

"That sounds like Peregrine," she said, and he returned her hand to her lap with ungentle haste.

"Don't, for God's sake, go weaving your romantic fancies around my brother and expect him to live up to legendary tradition," he snapped with a return of the old impatience.

"Oh, I don't," she said, already half asleep and impervious to ill-humour. "I don't think Perry's a true unicorn . . . he hasn't got blue eyes . . ."

"H-m . . ." he grunted. "Time we were going home. They'll have finished supper, I'm afraid, but Bella will find us something, and I'll attend to that hand properly before you go to bed."

He did not drive on immediately, but let the engine idle as he turned towards her suddenly and put one hand under her chin, tilting her face up to his. Her eyes flew open, but she could not see his expression very well in the darkness that had fallen, then he bent his head and kissed her very gently.

"That's to show you I have another side," he said, and would have let her go, but her arms wound round his neck and she was offering her mouth again.

"Why, Laura . . ." he murmured softly, and would have drawn her closer, but a noisy sports car shot by them, the angry popping of its exhaust disrupting the stillness and the delicate nuance of the moment.

"Perry evidently returning a little the worse for wear," he said a shade grimly, watching the car's tail-lights disappear up the road in erratic arcs and curves, and put his own car into motion.

The next day the household appeared to return to normal with the disregard for recent disturbances which could still astonish Laura. Peregrine, if he was suffering from a hangover, showed no sign of it, and was his usual boastful self. Dominic, though he looked a little tired, seemed only to be occupied with the many outside jobs about the place which a week's holiday from the works would allow them to catch up on, and even Cleo had shed her bitter moodiness and resumed her lazy rôle as mistress of the house.

"It's extraordinary how they all seem able to throw things off as if they had never happened," Laura said to Bella, realising, even as she spoke, that she now classed Cleo with the dark Trevaynes.

"It would make for a very uncomfortable domestic life if they did not, dear child," Bella replied with unanswerable logic. "It has not occurred to you, I suppose, that it might be an alien element among us that sparks off these little disturbances?"

"Are you, by any chance, suggesting that *I'm* this alien element?" Laura asked with such astonishment that Bella shook her head at her in faint reproof.

"But of course. You might think that it's your cousin who creates tension with her airs and graces and strong sexual appeal, but she's too like them to score by being unexpected. It's natural, of course, that Perry should be attracted, for he's very like Troy in his tastes, but Dom remembers his mother, and she was not unlike you."

"What was she like — Mrs. Trevayne?" Laura asked eagerly, as she had once asked Dominic, and Bella replied as he had:

"Gentle and undemanding — a little like you, dear child, as I remember, in her fondness for legends and day-dreaming. Zachary, of course, was much too old for her — he could have been her father — and he never, you know, understood a woman's needs other than the physical. She found her solace in books and verse, and Dom, of course . . . he was the only one she had, you see, to share her private dreams and follies with, and that's made him different from the other two."

"Yes I see. He missed her very much, didn't he?"

"Well, he was eight when she died and old for his age — old enough to have passed the formative years. Don't the Jesuits say 'Give me a child until he's seven' — I forget the rest of it," Bella finished, and Laura said, reflectively:

"I suppose that's what Dominic feels about Nicky. You know, of course, he wants to bring him up here."

"Oh, yes. Dom feels very strongly that the boy's

mixed blood will prove a dangerous heritage if there's no firm hand to guide him."

"Mixed blood?"

"Well, your cousin is no more stable than Troy was, dear child, you must agree."

"You don't like Cleo, do you, Bella?" Laura said, but Bella replied with faint surprise:

"I don't feel vey strongly either way, dear child, since she will not be among us for much longer."

"But, Bella," Laura began, "you must know, surely — I — I think they mean to marry — to settle the problem of Nicky that way, you know."

"Really, dear child? Oh, I don't think that would settle anything — unicorns, you see, are not for her," said Bella, and drifted away.

Really, reflected Laura a little crossly, Bella could be most exasperating at times, but the mention of unicorns reminded her that her hand felt no less painful, despite Dominic's professional dressing last night, and was beginning to swell a little.

"Do you think it's getting gangrene or something?" she asked him quite seriously later in the day, and although he replied with solemn ridicule that undoubtedly the hand would have to be amputated, when he took the bandage off he said she had better see a doctor.

"I'll drive you down to St. Mewan after tea. You probably need an antibiotic injection," he said, but in the end it was Peregrine who took her, a Peregrine behaving once more very like a spoilt child.

He had, when Nicky had come down for tea, made a great play for the boy's attention, never doubting he could recapture the old allegiance with a few jokes and a conspiratorial incitement to mischief, but Nicky would not go near him, sidling round the tea-table to sit as close as he could to Dominic. All Peregrine's blandishments met with the same sullen lack of response until Dominic told him rather sharply to leave the child alone; but Peregrine could leave nothing alone that savoured of personal defeat, and Nicky suddenly and very disastrously found his tongue.

"I *hate* my Uncle Perry!" he announced to the

room at large. "He's cruel and wicked and — he's not my unimecorn any more!"

Cleo laughed and even Bella smiled, but Peregrine, displaying the injured pride of a schoolboy made to look ridiculous in front of his elders, hurled a cup across the table at Nicky, who shrieked as it smashed in pieces, and flung himself upon Dominic in a torrent of tears.

"Oh, for God's sake, don't behave like a child yourself, Perry!" Dominic snapped, then lifted the boy on to his knee and set about soothing him, while Laura said quickly:

"Perry can take me. Don't miss your chance, Dominic. You've got him where you want him, and it won't hurt for once to turn a blind eye."

He frowned, then smiled at her a little ruefully and obediently hoisted the child to his shoulders for a piggy-back up the stairs.

To Laura's relief, Cleo decided to go into St. Mewan with them for the ride. She was glad not to be the sole recipient of Peregrine's sulks and grumbles and thankfully left them to their sparring while she waited her turn in the surgery. By the time she came out again they appeared to have reached an amicable understanding and dropped her back at Penzion, then went off to spend the rest of the evening together.

Laura went up to the nursery to relieve Dominic of his charge and found them both happily engaged in building a house of cards on the floor, at least Dominic was patiently building, and Nicky, with unholy shrieks of joy, was blowing it down.

"I never get a chance," Dominic complained, getting to his feet. "This terrible north wind blows my house down before I reach the second storey."

"Story!" shouted Nicky, who was very quick on word association.

"In a minute. What had the medico to say about that hand, Laura?"

"He thought I would live," she smiled. "No, seriously — he said the wound had gone a bit septic but an injection would put that right, and I will say it feels better already."

"*Story!*" insisted Nicky, dancing up and down with impatience. and Dominic picked him up and sat him on the deep, half-circular window-seat covered with a patched and faded nursery chintz.

"Well now, suppose we get Moo-moo to tell us both a story," he said, and Laura sat down on the opposite half of the semicircle to them and folded her hands.

"Well, once upon a time . . ." she began, and he sat watching her, remembering this was a favourite and characteristic pose of her hers. Thus had she sat on a stool in the book-room, her feet neatly together and her hands folded in her lap like a little girl She looked like a little girl now with the light brown hair curving about her neck, and the great, clear eyes as wide and solemn as Nicky's.

He was not paying any great attention to the story, which appeared to concern the abortive nuptials of a fearsome-sounding prince rejoicing in the name of Lindworm. who gobbled up a succession of brides on their wedding nights. The unfortunate gentleman was apparently under a spell, for all came right in the end when the third bride, who clearly had more *nous* than the other two, bade him slough his skins, of which he had ten, and he was disenchanted.

The story seemed to come to a rather abrupt end with Laura looking slightly pink, and Nicky said accusingly:

"You left out the part when she had to take him in her arms and kiss him when he was still all ugly and slimy. Moo-moo. It's the importantest part of *all,* because if she *hadn't* kissed him when he was horrible and scary. the spell wouldn't have *worked!*"

"Yes, well . . ." said Laura rather lamely, and Dominic directed a steady gaze on her faintly embarrassed face and tried to keep the amusement out of his eyes.

"Very remiss of Moo-moo to omit the proper ending," he agreed solemnly. "I think she thought my feelings might be hurt."

"Because of your face?" the boy enquired with renewed interest as, tired of sitting still, he began to slide off the window-seat.

"Well, you found my face scary once, young man."

" '*Course* I didn't! Not when I knew it was a pirate made that funny mark with his cutlass — besides, you're a unimecorn now, and that's different," Nicky retorted.

"Oh, Laura . . .!" Dominic murmured with tender ridicule, and she smiled reluctantly.

"Yes, I suppose it was rather silly of me," she admitted. "I don't know why I should have imagined you'd be sensitive about your scar, which is really rather distinguished in a buccaneering sort of way."

He laughed and said:

"You are very absurd, and very endearing."

"Endearing?"

"Does that surprise you? I'm beginning to wonder, you know, if I've been misled on certain matters." Then he took her suddenly by the wrist and jerked her round to face him.

"I want you to stay," he said abruptly. "In spite of your threat yesterday to spit in my eye!"

She considered, with that thoughtful solemnity she had at times, and said:

"I was in a temper then. I'll stay, of course, as long as Cleo needs me here."

"Thank you," he said gravely. "Your cousin's plans are, I think, nearly decided on."

"And they are the same as yours?"

"I hope so."

She looked away, finding it difficult to sustain that very blue regard for long, and sighed. The transformed burrows seemed to lose their magic, and the old hound, Rowley, slowly crossing the lawn dragging his hindquarters, stabbed her sharply with the sad reminder of the brief transience of life.

"Poor old dog — he hasn't got much longer, I'm afraid," Dominic said, his eyes following her, and she shivered.

"Your heart's too tender," he said a little roughly.

"Life will hurt you, Laura, and so will people unless you grow a protective skin."

"Have you found that?"

"Oh, yes, but with me it has to work in reverse, you see. Like your bedevilled Prince Lindworm, one has to learn to slough the skin," he replied unexpectedly. "I sloughed one last night when you so surprised me up there on the headland."

"It's not," she replied, as she had on another occasion, "very fair to remind me of a — an indiscretion. I was not at all myself."

"Weren't you? Was I, after all, only a substitute for Perry?" He spoke too lightly for her to read anything other than a kindly offer of escape from embarrassment into the casual question, and remembering Cleo's hints and even his own upon occasion, she answered as lightly:

"Perhaps. I'd better start getting Nicky ready for bed. It's long past his time."

"I see," he said with a complete change of voice. He was already on his feet, and stood for a moment looking down at her, tall and lean and hard, once more the dark stranger withdrawn behind those unexplained defences. She put out a tentative hand as if she would detain him, but he turned abruptly on his heel and left the room.

The days of that holiday week were filled with the casual comings and goings of the household, but it was scarcely a holiday atmosphere.

Going upstairs one morning, Laura passed by Cleo's room.

The door was open and Cleo herself appeared to be having an unaccustomed urge to sort out her clothes. Dresses were piled on the bed, shoes thrown all over the floor, and Cleo herself looked untidy and decidedly cross.

"What are you doing?" Laura asked, poking her head round the door.

"Finding little jobs for you, darling; broken shoulder-straps and missing buttons. You might as well come in and help me sort. God! What a state my things are in — they look like a rag-bag!"

"Well, you never hang anything up, so what can you expect?" Laura observed with that bright little air of practicality which amused Dominic but annoyed Cleo.

"You might," she went on good-temperedly, "have given me your mending as things wore out instead of in one great lump. What do you want done first?"

"The lot. I shall be going away quite soon," said Cleo casually, and Laura stiffened.

"When?"

"Oh, in a week or so — possibly sooner. It depends."

It depended on Dominic's arrangements, Laura presumed, experiencing a sudden little sick stab of dismay that time at last was running out and this was the reckoning.

"Well, let me know your dates as soon as you can," she said, striving to sound matter-of-fact and casual. "I shall have to give the hostel good notice of my return or they'll be booked up."

Cleo raised a delicate eyebrow, and settled more comfortably into her chair.

"Oh, will you be coming too?"

"Naturally. You'll need help with Nicky on the journey, anyway."

"Nicky's staying here."

"Oh!" Laura sat down on the bed, feeling a little weak. Cleo had, she knew, been closeted in the book-room with Dominic for some time after supper last night, and evidently a decision had been reached then.

"I understood from Dom you had agreed to stop on and look after Nicky," Cleo said.

"I agreed to stop on as long as you need me here," Laura replied.

"Then you must sort that one out with Dom, mustn't you, darling?"

"Cleo, have things worked out as you hoped . . . have you settled Nicky's future?"

"Things seldom work out as you hope, my dear, as you'll find out for yourself, but yes, things have worked very well, and yes, I've settled Nicky's future."

"And your own?" Laura did not know why the question she wanted to ask stuck in her throat, unless it was for fear that once the answer was given the frail solace of a foolish dream would be gone, and Cleo, too, seemed in no greater mind to be more definite.

"Mine? My future has always been in the lap of the gods, darling, and I like it that way," she said with her lazy, cat-like smile.

"But you'll be coming back here?"

"Oh, yes, I'll be coming back, my transparent little simpleton, so don't start getting ideas above your station again."

And that, thought Laura, of course answered the question. Naturally Cleo would be going away for a time if for no other reason than to collect a trousseau. She gathered up a pile of mending and took it along to the nursery.

CHAPTER TEN

THE WEEK had nearly ended, and Laura, feeling aggrieved that no one had troubled to take a day off and suggest one last expedition to send her away with pleasant memories of Cornwall, said to Dominic:

"Couldn't you — I mean, if I'm going so soon, I would like — I haven't even seen the quarry yet, let alone the places Bella promised me that day of our picnic."

"Are you going?" he said, with that infuriating suggestion of polite surprise. "I understood you had agreed to stop on."

"I agreed to stay as long as Cleo needed me here, but as she's going soon—"

"Is that all she told you?"

"Yes — except that she'd be coming back."

"I see. Well, Nicky will need you in the meantime, won't he?"

"I suppose so. Dominic—"

"Don't fuss about things that don't concern you, Laura. If, as you say, you agreed to stay so long as your cousin needed you here, she will obviously need you until she can make other arrangements for the boy, won't she?" he said, dismissing the matter, but Peregrine was more co-operative.

"What a shame, poor Miss Bread-and-butter! Well, what about tomorrow? I'll run you round to see sights if you'll say where you'd like to go."

"It doesn't matter," she said. "I would like to have seen the quarry before I go, but that wouldn't be much of an outing for you."

"Why not?" he said. "We could take the brat and, between us, win him back to his poor Uncle Perry, who's been too long in the doghouse. Yes?"

"All right," said Laura, not very enthusiastically. Peregrine, she knew, had been absurdly riled by Nicky's continued refusal to make friends again, but the boy at least provided an excuse for the curtailment of unwelcome attentions.

167

"Why don't you come too, my pretty?" Peregrine said to Cleo the next afternoon when they were about to start, but when she replied languidly that perhaps she would, just for the ride, he said rather quickly:

"Think again, then. Three's company, etc. We don't of course, count your son and heir, who'll probably be sick, anyway."

"Why did you suggest it, then?" she snapped, not unreasonably, but her eyes rested on Laura with a distinctly jealous gleam which he saw and enjoyed.

"For possibly the same reason that you deserve, yourself, for evening up the score," he said spitefully, and they at once became embroiled in one of their quarrels.

Laura withdrew out of earshot with the boy, wishing she had declined the invitation. Nicky had needed very tactful persuasion when he had understood it was his Uncle Perry and not his Uncle Dom in charge of the expedition, and the heated words being flung back and forth at the moment only seemed to be proof that both protagonists were jealous. If Laura felt surprise that she could cause her glamorous cousin a moment's uneasiness where another was concerned, the knowledge gave her no satisfaction. She only knew a fleeting compassion for Cleo, who, though her desires were so plainly centred on one man, was still prepared to make do with another because that union paid off best.

The quarrel seemed to have abated, and Laura pushed the boy forward again in time to hear Peregrine say:

"Don't be such a clot, you little fool! Do you think I care one way or the other? I've a few scores to settle up, that's all, and this is as good a way as any."

"Am I supposed to guess what's in your tiny mind?" Cleo drawled in her husky voice. "A rather dull inspection of the Zion Works doesn't sound very promising to me."

"Nor is it, my sweet, except that I'll have the brat back where I want him by the time we return — but

168

you can keep on guessing — and keep Big Brother guessing, too, if you're clever."

Nicky had created a diversion by sitting down on the gravel, and expressing a desire to stop at home, so most of the rather meaningless little exchange was lost, but as Laura lifted the reluctant child into the car and took her place beside him, she felt a twinge of uneasiness.

"Why don't you come, Cleo?" she asked her cousin impulsively, but Cleo, apparently restored to her normal indifference, shook her head and shrugged.

"Oh, no darling — two's company and three's none, as Perry has just pointed out — besides, I've other fish to fry," she said, and went back into the house.

The irrational disquiet Laura had experienced as they drove away was soon dispelled in the novelty of having the intricacies of quarrying and the production of china clay explained. Peregrine was an excellent guide, and when Nicky tired they left him playing happily in a sheltered sandpit. Laura was fascinated by the filter process, and the clay stream flowing through the mica drays like a fabulous river of clotted cream, but the deserted buildings and the gaunt skeletons of idle machinery depressed her.

"Oughtn't we to be going? There seems to be a mist coming down, and Nicky will be getting cold in that sandpit," she said, and his smile was suddenly a little unpleasant.

"I'll go and fetch him," he said. "In the meantime, my pretty Laura, I'm going to lock you here till I get back, just in case you go falling into one of the quarries. Be seeing you!"

He had slipped out of the door and locked it behind him before she had time to recover her breath and expostulate, and she ran to one of the windows to watch which direction he took. He appeared to be going towards the sandpit, and presently she saw him returning with the boy, but though she could not imagine why he had seen fit to play such a childish trick on her, she was not alarmed; but the mist rolling up from the sea and across the moor seemed to be thickening rather rapidly. She had read about these west country fogs which could suddenly blot out the countryside in an impenetrable blanket, and decided they must get the boy back to Penzion at once, before transport could become dangerous.

Nicky, though he was reduced to tears, looked cold and frightened, and when Peregrine put him down, he ran to Laura and began to whimper.

"Why have you locked the door again?" she said angrily, going down on her knees beside the boy. "This rather feeble joke's gone far enough, and I want to leave."

Peregrine propped his back against the door and grinned at her.

"It's no joke, my sweet, and we're not leaving," he said.

"Oh now, really, Perry! You're too old to start playing cops and robbers!" she exclaimed, refusing to be alarmed. "If we don't go now, it soon won't be safe to drive."

"Very true, my pretty. That, of course, was a stroke of good fortune I hadn't foreseen, so the gods are clearly on my side. I must say I admire your refusal to panic, but you always were a bit of a surprise in that way, weren't you? That literal mind again, I shouldn't wonder."

She lifted Nicky on to one of the bunks and covered him with a blanket, then turned and regarded Peregrine, her arms folded in the traditional attitude of any nanny determined to stand no nonsense.

"My literal mind is unimpressed by silly posturing," she told him coolly. "You can't keep us here all night, and if we don't go now you'll find we're stranded."

"That hardly matters, for I'd every intention of keeping you here all night, fog or no fog, so put that in your stubborn little pipe and smoke it."

"But why — why?" she said. "I can't see any point, unless you're hoping to make Cleo jealous, which I may add, is hardly likely."

"Don't you think so? You've given your self-assured cousin cause for that in more ways than one, or didn't you know?"

"Stuff and nonsense!" she exclaimed loudly, and he put his head on one side.

"Alice, of course . . ." he said, sounding delighted with his own cleverness, "that's who you must always have reminded me of. I wonder if Dom's spotted it."

"If you know your *Alice,* then you'll remember how *she* dealt with people who needed putting in their places. 'Who cares for *you?'* said Alice. 'You're nothing but a pack of cards!' " quoted Laura. "And that's all you are, Peregrine Trevayne — all the Trevaynes, probably, with their high-stepping opinions and — and cardboard histrionics — nothing but a pack of cards!"

"Well!" said Peregrine in genuine astonishment, then burst out laughing. Nicky, feeling safe and cosy again in his blanket, recognising a story-telling note in Moo-moo's voice, laughed too, but Laura, having relieved her outraged feelings and, as she thought, cut Peregrine neatly down to size, said on a coaxing note:

"Come on, Perry, you've had your fun. Let's go home."

A softer plea, however, merely stiffened him. A Laura quite unshaken by a possible threat to her virtue was no fun at all, but a pleading Laura already in love with a man who she imagined cared nothing for her was a different cup of tea.

"Well now," he said, swaggering across to her and pushing her down on to one of the bunks, "it's time you got wise to yourself, my dear. I've had this all planned since Big Brother socked me one in the pub. I told him I'd make him sorry for that — remember? At first I thought I'd just snatch the kid and disappear for a few days while Brother Dom sweated in uncertainty, then when you begged for a nice little outing to see the sights, I thought this was a better idea. True Dominic will only have to sweat for one night instead of several, but one night is quite long enough to sweat to some tune when a young girl and her imperilled virtue are involved."

"This all sounds very picturesque and melodramatic," she said with cool contempt. "But can you really carry pure spite to these lengths?"

"Troy did."

"And is Troy to be your criterion for behaviour all your life?"

"Ah! Now you're sounding like prim Miss Prunes-and-prisms again! You won't feel so smug by tomorrow morning, my girl."

"Oh, really, Perry! I may be young and inexperienced, but I'm not ignorant. I've always understood that rape is virtually impossible unless the victim is partially willing," she said, and he looked faintly surprised.

"Well, what d'you know! Our bread-and-butter miss talking glibly about such sordid things as rape as if it were of no more consequence than stubbing your toe!"

"Neither it is, I imagine, if one keeps one's head and remembers to kick," she retorted, but even as she spoke, she had a mental picture of her Auntie Flo's look of horror at such outspokenness, and felt herself blushing.

"Well!" he exclaimed. "I'm glad to see you can still blush!" The predatory overlord's notions of his ewe lamb's defenceless innocence would be slightly shattered, I feel. Still, he won't be aware of that tonight, will he?"

"Don't call him that," snapped Laura, lapsing momentarily into childish crossness. "That joke's already gone sour on him — and on me, too, Perry, I can understand your adolescent tit-for-tat idiocy in staging some silly stunt over the boy because, for once, Dominic's taken something from you and you don't like it; but *this* stupid caper — Dominic's scarcely going to worry unduly, knowing I'm with the child."

He gave her a long, faintly incredulous look, and sat down beside her on the bunk.

"Are you so dumb you can't see the delicious irony of that?" he asked quite gently. "Sure, he won't sweat about the boy, but he's going to sweat his guts out wondering what's happening to you. Don't you understand I've got the two beings he wants for himself, and one night's hell is going to pay off a lot of old scores."

She sat very still and very small beside him, and she must have been holding her breath, for he heard the long quivering sound as she slowly released it.

"Didn't you really know?" he asked, curiously. "Weren't you feminine enough to see through all that protective lord of the manor stuff?"

"He treats me like a child," she said, too shaken to remember her present invidious position. "I thought he was — embarrassed because he guessed how I felt. He even warned me . . ."

"He was warning you against losing your heart to me, I don't doubt. He thought you'd fallen for me — Cleo saw to that."

She sat up very straight and her eyes grew wide with wonder as everything fell into place.

"Did Cleo plan this with you?" she asked, and he grinned back at her, tempted to prick that new-found bubble of happiness, just for the hell of it.

"Well, no — to give her her due she didn't," he replied. "She knew I was up to something and I don't fancy she would have had any compunction in getting her own back on Dom as the woman scorned, etc., but she didn't connive, if that's what you mean."

"I'm glad," said Laura. "I wouldn't like to think she cared so little for me after all these years. What do you mean by the woman scorned?"

"Well she meant to marry the lord and master, as I think you knew."

"I thought that was the arrangement they must have come to — for Nicky's sake, you know."

"Oh, yes, I got the set-up, and I played along with that for a time. You were very touching that night in the pub, Laura. You wanted to extract a promise from me to lay off once they were married, didn't you? Well, clever Cleo has settled for a very nice little pay-off, and if she's still clever tonight — who knows, I might take unwilling steps to the altar myself! It won't, incidentally, do the little bitch any harm to sweat a bit herself, and she won't know, will she, that you and I, in such circumstances, might possibly cut our losses and settle for each other?"

"Most unlikely," said Laura with a return to her first briskness. "When we don't return, Dominic will come and get us. Cleo knows where we are."

"Don't kid yourself!" laughed Peregrine. "Have you looked at the weather? Dom will be as helpless as the next man to rescue his beloved from a fate worse than death; no one but a raving lunatic would venture out in this, and Dom knows these fogs."

Her eyes went to the window. She had been so intent on Peregrine's extraordinary revelations that she had paid no attention to the weather, except to be aware that the long, barrack-like room had darkened to an impression of twilight, but she saw now the impenetrable blanket of fog pressing against the window, and the swirling little wreaths of mist drifting in through every crack and cranny and hovering over the rows of bunks like smoke.

"All right!" she said, sliding off the bunk and going to Nicky, who had already fallen asleep on his. "So we spend the night here and go hungry. It won't kill any of us."

"We won't go hungry. I've got a hamper of food in the boot of the car," Peregrine said, and to Laura it was the final irritant, the last, childish assurance that, for Peregrine, the whole fantastic scheme was just an excuse for a party. She came back to where he was still sitting on the bunk they had both occupied, and dealt him a stinging slap across the cheek.

"You," she said, "ought to have grown out of such nonsense by now. I may have seemed naïve to you with my schoolgirl fantasies of pirates and smugglers and pieces of eight, but you, with your mean and spiteful pride in turning out exactly like your unpleasant old father and your dead brother, seem to me never to have grown up at all."

She knew at once that she had misjudged her own powers as she saw his hand go to his cheek and the ugly look which came into his black, brilliant eyes.

"That," he said with a gentleness that was all the more alarming because he was not a gentle person, "is a thing you'll be sorry for before the night is out, my dear. You have far more attraction for me in a belligerent mood, Laura, I'll admit, but — for that slap — I think I must teach you a lesson. We've all the night before us, and once the brat is safely asleep in his bunk, who's to know what goes on in another part of this shack? You'd better let me get that hamper — you'll need strength as the night wears on, to put these foolish boasts of yours into practice."

At Penzion the afternoon had passed tediously for Cleo with nothing to do but laze around and regret that she had not insisted on being one of the party visiting the quarry. Perry, of course, had been up to something, judging by his parting shot before he drove off, but it was not until later that she began having certain uneasy doubts. To be jealous of the little cousin whose affections were already engaged elsewhere was, of course, absurd, but lately Perry had been throwing out hints that Laura's charms might be worth consideration, and although Cleo was pretty sure he was simply at his old game of playing hard to get, he was more than capable, if sufficiently goaded, of taking a girl he did not want simply to spite the lot of them. And Laura? Well, she wouldn't be the first young star-crossed innocent to be caught on the rebound and have regrets too late.

Tea-time came and went, but Cleo had it alone. Dominic looked in about half-past five to enquire whether the others were back yet, and frowned when told they were not.

"The weather's getting a bit thick," he said. "Perry will surely have had the sense to start back before the roads get tricky. He knows what these fogs can be like."

"Well, it'll probably take a bit of time if he has to crawl," Cleo said indifferently. She was unused to fogs where there was no city lighting to aid the motorist, neither did she appreciate the dangers of a moorland road that could lead the unwary into a bog or over the cliff's edge.

As time went on, however, and the little party still

failed to return, she began to grow restless. She did not for a moment share Dominic's anxiety lest an accident had befallen them, for she thought she knew, now, just what Peregrine had in mind when he had said this was as good a way as any of settling old scores. Not only did he mean to pay back his brother for imagined grievances, but her as well. She had driven him too far, blowing first hot, then cold, and making a play for Dominic to goad him into thoughts of marriage himself. She had made it too plain that she was willing to marry the elder brother if necessary, providing the old affair could continue as before, and had been no less surprised than Perry was himself when he had finally admitted that he drew the line at that.

At seven o'clock, Dominic abandoned his labours, saying the weather was now too thick for comfort, but several times he walked down to the gates to look up the road as anxious people will, even though knowing the errand to be fruitless.

"Can't you ring up? The place is on the telephone, surely?" said Cleo impatiently.

"I did so an hour ago, but got no reply," he answered.

"So they're on their way and it'll probably take them hours."

"You don't really think that, any more than I do."

"Well then, what should one think? Someone would have answered the phone if they're still there."

"Not necessarily. The telephone's in the office and there are other more comfortable places to bed down if you're stranded."

"Bed down?"

"A figure of speech, of course," he said smoothly. "We boast a quite comfortable bunk-house for the men on night-shift. There would be no need to suffer any very great inconvenience."

She did not care very much for the way he was looking at her and her eyes slid away from his.

"Well, surely Perry would have rung us himself if they were stranded," she said uneasily.

"Would he?"

He poured her another drink, then helped himself and went to stand at the window with his back to her. There was little daylight left, owing to the fog, and the lights had already been turned on in the tea-room where they were waiting until Bella should be ready with supper.

There was a long silence between them, then Dominic tossed off his whisky, put down the empty glass, and was suddenly across the room in a few swift strides.

"Hadn't you better come clean, Cleo?" he said quite gently.

"What do you mean?" she temporised, but she looked frightened.

"You know they're there, don't you? Did you and Perry cook this up between you — each getting your own back on me, but for different reasons?"

"No — no. I swear I knew nothing, Dom," she said, and now that the affair was out in the open she could give voice to her own misgivings. "Perry muttered something about settling old scores and this being as good a way as any, but I didn't suspect till later what he was probably planning. Yes, I think they're still there; I don't think Perry ever had any intention of coming back tonight. Bella says a lot of food has gone from the larder. Dom, can't you go and fetch them, or at least get as far as the Works and spend the night there with them?"

"To play the unwanted protector and be brushed off for high-handed interference?" he said with bitter irony, and she realised that her own doubts and regrets had made her forget that he must imagine that Laura would hardly be an unwilling party to anything Perry might propose.

"Oh, Dom, you *fool!*" she cried, driven at last by her own jealousy to the truth. "Laura doesn't care a rap for Perry! I know I gave you to understand otherwise, but if you hadn't been so blind you'd have have seen it for yourself long ago. The poor little ninny is sick with love for you, but she thought you were warning her off with all this kid-glove handling as if she was a half-witted child."

For a moment she thought he was going to strike her, so lividly did the scar stand out as the skin tightened in anger across the bones of his dark face, but when he spoke it was with that quiet control which she had come to recognise as more dangerous than his brother's fireworks.

"My kid-glove handling, as you call it, might have borne fruit if you hadn't lied and deliberately misled me as, I suppose, you also misled Laura. You're a bitch and a tramp, Cleo, and quite without any moral decency."

"Hard words won't hurt me now," she flung back at him, brazening things out as the only possible defence in a tight corner. "I wanted you myself, and they say all's fair in love and war."

"Oh no, you always wanted Perry, but you wanted marriage, too. You're greedy, Cleo. When Perry wouldn't play, you settled for me, thinking that way you'd have the best of both worlds, didn't you? You weren't very clever, my dear; if you'd made marriage your price, as you tried to do with me over Nicky, instead of plunging into an affair with him, you might have got what you wanted."

The tears welled up in her eyes, not tears of shame or even remorse, but of self-disgust at having bungled a project through a wanton excess of physical desire and over-self-confidence.

"Oh, I know I've been a fool," she said, "but you got under my skin with all this everlasting concern for youth and innocence, with the implication that I could look after myself — Laura, too, with her naïve gullibility and her bread-and-butter ways."

"In other words you were jealous that any man could prefer the despised little cousin to you," he said quite gently, and she gave him a wry smile.

"Yes, I suppose I was," she said frankly. "I've never, you see, imagined there could be any competition between us, and neither has she."

"It's you who are naïve, not Laura. She has a quality you wouldn't begin to understand," he said, and there was just a hint of compassion in his smile which she saw with surprise.

"Dom," she said, stretching out a hand to him, "you've been generous to me over Nicky. It's not too late for me to put things right for you."

"I'll put my own affairs right, when the time comes, without your help, thank you, Cleo," he said with a touch of the old Trevayne hauteur, and she said a little spitefully:

"Of course, it may already be too late. Perry says virgins are very delectable bait, and Perry's no sluggard when it comes to taking what he wants, and then throwing it away. Girls, too, if they imagine their affections rejected, will turn to someone else for false comfort."

"I've not overlooked any of those things," he replied, "but it's a little late to make mischief now. Whatever the outcome of this night's work, my feelings will remain the same."

The naked pain which she glimpsed for a moment in his eyes provoked an animal instinct in her to tear down and destroy something which she could not understand, and she said with derisive scorn:

"Oh, I'm sure you'd be willing to take over Perry's leavings, just as you would have taken over Troy's. What a pity you never seem able to make first base."

He did hit her then, a stinging smack across the cheek with the flat of his hand which sent the blood tingling under her skin, and he stood over her with such dark passion in his face that she shrank back against the cushions.

"I don't apologise for that because it's the only sort of treatment you understand, and you'll doubtless get plenty from Perry if you ever bring him up to scratch," he said. "Now, you can listen to my ultimatum for the last time, for I shan't bother to repeat it. Last night we came to terms. You were willing to hand over the boy in return for a specified sum, and signed an agreement to that effect. I will add a further condition to get rid of you and your particular brand of poison. If Perry still wants to be bought out of the business I'll somehow raise the money to do so, and what arrangement the pair of you come to after that I neither care nor want to know. But you will be out of my house by tomorrow — understand? My lawyers will see that things are tied up legally as soon as possible, but in the meantime, I no longer want you under my roof — yes, Bella?"

For almost the first time Cleo welcomed the interruption. She was scared, but also quite genuinely at a loss to understand how she had failed to measure up to the familiar Trevayne tradition. She would end up, she knew, with one of those upsetting crying jags, and there would be no Laura, this time, to sit up half the night and soothe with soft words and cool compresses.

"I wondered what you wanted to do about eating, Dom," Bella was saying. "I have a stew in the oven, but I don't think it's much use waiting any longer for the others, do you?"

"No, Bella, no use at all. They won't be back tonight," Dominic said.

"No, I thought not. Do not agitate yourself, dear boy, on that account. Perry is not a true unicorn, you know," Bella said, and went calmly back to the kitchen to dish up.

For Dominic it was a long and weary night of mental torment, and the no less agonising state of enforced impotence, for there was nothing he could do until the fog lifted. He sat up listening to the clock strike hour after hour with the dragging slowness which time has for those who must wait, isolated in the eerie silence which fog brings, when night sounds are stilled and no bird stirs. Bella sat with him, replenishing the fire from time to time, but neither of them spoke much, nor did their thoughts once go to Cleo, sleeping at last in her bed upstairs; perhaps for both of them she had already ceased to exist. It was nearly five when Dominic went again to the window to look out, and this time he drew back the curtains with fresh decisiveness.

"It's clearing," he said. "In a very little while we can get going."

Bella came and stood beside him and they watched the dawn breaking through the curtain of mist which every so often swirled and parted sufficiently to reveal the dim shapes of shrubs and the stone seats on the terrace beyond. Presently the light began to change. The sun was coming up and, as the first rosy rays grew stronger and the fog started to disperse with a heartening speed, Dominic told Bella to go and fetch her coat. It was she who had decided she should go with him, for, she said, someone should be there to take charge of the little boy while other matters were attended to.

"Dear Bella," he had said affectionately, "nothing ever surprises you, does it? I suppose you've known about my understandable stupidity all along?"

"Oh yes, dear boy," she replied. "Sometimes your blindness afforded me great annoyance, but then I chided myself for lack of faith when all the portents were there for those who cared to accept them."

"Accept what portents?" he asked, because he liked to tease her, but she only smiled that rather baffling smile and said:

"You know very well, dear boy."

He felt immeasurably tired as he turned the car on to the cliff road with Bella beside him, but the headland air was sweet and fresh and, even at this early hour, the sun had warmth enough to ease the tautness of his skin. By the time they had reached the quarry gates only pockets of mist still hung about in the hollows and declivities in the moor; dew sparkled on everything, and the sky was a tender arc of duck's egg blue; it was going to be a beautiful day.

Dominic drove to the bunk-house, sounding a blast on his horn, and presently the door opened and Peregrine stood there, hands on hips and legs aggressively apart.

"Well, well, well! The tardy deliverer just several hours too late," he said as his brother got stiffly from the car.

"Where are they?" Dominic barked, his tiredness forgotten in a returning wave of last night's fury.

"In there, asleep," Peregrine grinned, with a jerk of the head behind him. "Why don't you go in and have a look? Your ewe lamb appears charming in sleep; on second thoughts, though, I shouldn't wake her. She's had a rather exhausting night, which, of course, was only to be expected. Isn't it a beautiful morning? So—" He choked on the unfinished sentence as his brother took him by the collar and yanked him off the low wooden platform that ran all round the building.

"You've been spoiling for a fight for a very long time, and now you're going to get it," Dominic said.

"History repeating itself? Same place, same bone of contention," sneered Peregrine, still on one knee in the soft white china clay dust where he had sprawled.

"I don't think so. We'll fight fair this time, but we'll fight bloodily too. I've had about as much as I'll stand from you, Perry. Get up and defend yourself." He jerked his brother to his feet by the collar again, and surprised a most unfamiliar look of sheepishness in the black eyes that looked bloodshot in the early morning light.

"I'm not fighting you, Dom," Peregrine said unexpectedly, and the insolence had dropped away from him.

"What in hell are you up to now? Gone chickenhearted when it comes to a showdown?" Dominic said roughly.

"No. Your terrifying ewe lamb who, I'm beginning to suspect, was sired by a tiger and not a mild old tup, has already defeated me," he said, but before he had finished speaking his brother had knocked him down.

He sat there, nursing a tender jaw, but made no move to get up and strike a blow for himself, and Dominic slowly lowered his own fists.

"What were you saying?" he asked. The torment of those waiting hours had bitten too deeply to permit of reasoning as yet, but faced with this inexplicable refusal to fight, he felt the anger begin to drain out of him.

"I was saying, when you so rudely interrupted," Peregrine replied, "that I had already been defeated, and made to eat humble pie at the point of a gun, so to speak. Ask her yourself — there she is!"

Dominic turned and saw Laura standing on the narrow platform, the rosy tint of morning touching her pale face with warmth. She had clearly been roused from sleep, and standing there in her crumpled dress, with her hair tousled and her drowsy eyes blinking against the sunlight, she looked like a surprised little girl, not yet wholly awake.

"Laura . . . are you all right?" Dominic asked very quietly, and at the sound of his voice she seemed to shake the sleep from her, and the colour crept up under her skin.

"Of course, Dominic, quite all right," she replied with her customary sedateness. "You mustn't fight, you know."

"See what I mean?" remarked Peregrine from the ground. "Your ewe lamb has salutary methods of dealing with would-be seducers — no struggles and maidenly shrieks of pleas for mercy — just practical, unconcerned reasonings that would damp the most ardent spirit, and a nursery lecture on good behaviour to boot! She's quite a gal! Why don't you fling yourself into his arms, Miss Bread-and-butter? He has, after all, come to save you from a fate worse than death, albeit unnecessarily as things have turned out, but he's earned some reward, don't you think?"

She took no notice of him, but just stood there staring at Dominic, her colour mounting in waves until at last she held both hands to her face in embarrassment.

Peregrine had got to his feet, and he gave his brother a hesitant slap on the back.

"She's not quite sure of you, you see," he said. "I spilled the beans for her, just as I don't doubt Cleo has for you, but she's never actually heard you say the magic words. Well, I'll be off home for a bath and a shave, which, by the way, you look as if you could do with yourself. Oh, just for the record — had you by any chance found yourself wedded to the wrong lady, I — I wasn't prepared to carry on that affair while I still broke your bread. So long!"

He walked away without looking back, and presently the sound of his sports engine, emitting noises like a last defiant rudeness, shattered the early morning silence, then diminished with a receding whine into the distance.

Silence closed down on the quarry again, and the isolation seemed complete. Bella must have slipped into the bunk-house unobserved, but Laura still stood there, silent and waiting, and Dominic went to her and circled her waist with his two hands.

"Laura . . .?" he said, and there was a hesitant question in the way he spoke her name. As she stood on the little platform, her eyes were level with his, and she slowly took his face between her hands.

"Was it bad — the waiting?" she asked, seeing the tiredness in his eyes and the endearing spattering of white threads exposed in his uncombed black hair.

"Yes, it was bad," he told her gravely. "You are, you see, very precious to me."

"Then it's really true?"

"That I love you, my dearest dear? Yes, it's really true."

"Not just another of my foolish whimsies?"

"No. Are you going to be hard to convince, Miss Mouse?"

"I don't think so. It's never hard to be convinced of something you've wanted badly," she said, and his hands tightened on her waist and he swung her suddenly down to the ground, and close up against him.

"What fools we've been, my silly sweetheart," he said a little roughly, and she answered back with that familiar, engaging refusal to be taken for granted:

"There was some excuse for me, since I'm not very experienced in love, but you should have known better, being the dark Trevayne and lord of all you survey."

"So I should. Predatory overlords should, in any case, take what they want, regardless of the wishes of others. Isn't that how you thought of me?"

"Only at first."

"Oh, no, allow me to correct you. At first you thought I was the devil," he told her severely, and she laid two fingers against his lips.

"Are you always going to treat me like a child that must be humoured?" she asked, and saw an uncharacteristic shyness touch the dark, unshaven face for an instant.

"No, my darling, but one's defences don't come tumbling down in a minute, having been painfully built up in the first place," he said. "We have to discover one another slowly. As for me — part of you will always remain the endearing child I first loved. Shall you mind?"

She rubbed her cheek against his, feeling its roughness, and felt, too, the roughness of his toiler's hands as they touched her flesh.

"No, I shan't mind. I'll mind nothing ever again so long as I'm with you," she said, before offering him her mouth, and the ardent pressure of her young breasts against him . . .

As he released her, the sun came up behind the tall burrows, turning them to gold, transforming even the ugly buildings and gaunt machinery to a fantasy of fleeting beauty.

"There's your magic working for you," Dominic said, and his own dark face was touched with that golden light. "Even the modern eyesores of commerce can borrow enchantment for a moment."

"Sloughing another skin, like Prince Lindworm?" she murmured reminiscently, but he shook his head at her and let that very blue, challenging regard of his dwell for a long moment on her upturned face before replying.

"No," he said with tenderness, "I think you've forgotten the unicorn."

"*Oh!*" Her eyes grew wide and her mouth began to curve in a slow smile of discovery.

" 'No sooner does he see the damsel . . .' " she quoted softly, " '. . . than he runs trustfully towards her . . . and so suffers himself to be captured . . .' "

You have just "experienced" a Harlequin romance novel. Like tens of millions of Harlequin readers throughout the world, you may wish to make romance fiction a pleasurable habit.

It's easy.

Twelve Harlequin romance titles are issued each month under two imprints: Harlequin Romances and Harlequin Presents. They are conveniently available in bookstores, supermarkets, chain and variety stores...wherever paperback books are sold.

What readers say about Harlequin romance fiction...

"I feel as if I am in a different world every time I read a Harlequin."

A.T.,* Detroit, Michigan

"Harlequins have been my passport to the world. I have been many places without ever leaving my doorstep."

P.Z., Belvedere, Illinois

"I like Harlequin books because they tell so much about other countries."

N.G., Rouyn, Quebec

"Your books offer a world of knowledge about places and people."

L.J., New Orleans, Louisiana

"Your books turn my...life into something quite exciting."

B.M., Baldwin Park, California

"Harlequins take away the world's troubles and for a while you can live in a world of your own where love reigns supreme."

L.S., Beltsville, Maryland

"Thank you for bringing romance back to me."

J.W., Tehachapi, California

"I find Harlequins are the only stories on the market that give me a satisfying romance with sufficient depth without being maudlin."

C.S., Bangor, Maine

"Harlequins are magic carpets...away from pain and depression...away to other people and other countries one might never know otherwise."

H.R., Akron, Ohio

*Names available on request

Harlequin understands...

the way you feel about love

Harlequin novels are stories of
people in love—people like you—
and all are beautiful romances,
set in exotic faraway places.

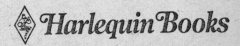

For more than 30 years, Harlequin has been publishing the very best in romantic fiction.

Today, Harlequin books are the world's best-selling paperback romances.